CRUEL PROMISE

CRUEL PROMISE

K.A. LINDE

DIAMOND GIRLS SERIES

Rock Hard | A Girl's Best Friend

In the Rough | Shine Bright

Under Pressure

TAKE ME DUET

Take Me for Granted | Take Me with You

STAND ALONE

Following Me

Hold the Forevers

FANTASY ROMANCE

BLOOD TYPE SERIES

Blood Type | Blood Match | Blood Cure

ASCENSION SERIES

The Affiliate | The Bound | The Consort

The Society | The Domina

ROYAL HOUSES

House of Dragons | House of Shadows

Cruel Promise
Copyright © 2020 by K.A. Linde
All rights reserved.

Visit my website at
www.kalinde.com

Cover Designer: Staci Hart
www.stacihartnovels.com
Editor: Unforeseen Editing
www.unforeseenediting.com

ISBN-13: 978-1948427487

WINTER

I

"Breathe. You can do this."

I bit my dark pink–painted lips, pushed open the door, and stepped into the chaos that was the Wisconsin state headquarters for Governor Woodhouse's presidential bid. It was everything I'd expected. Staff seated at cubicles, half-finished signs littered a table, an array of volunteers lined up in front of a row of computers, and the permeating smell of coffee.

I couldn't stop the excited smile from creeping onto my face. I was really here. I'd made it to Madison, and I was officially working for Governor Woodhouse—at a state office, no less. It was as if all of my dreams were finally coming true.

"You look lost," a guy said, stepping up with the biggest, most heart-stopping brown eyes I'd ever seen.

"A little," I admitted. "I'm Lark. I'm supposed to start working here today, I think."

His eyes brightened even further. "The new girl. Right. Toby said you'd be coming in today. He said that I'd be mentoring you." He stuck his hand out. "I'm Sam."

"Hi."

I shook his hand, lingering a second at the firm grasp and long musician's fingers. I drew back shyly. Something I was pretty sure I'd never been in my entire life. But the look on Sam's face was enough to make me forget who I was. That I was actually Larkin St. Vincent, heiress to St. Vincent's Enterprise, a multi-billion-dollar company headquartered in New York City. Not that I wanted anyone to know that here.

"Well, welcome to Madison. It's not New York—that's where you're from, right?" he asked, continuing without waiting for my answer, "But I think you'll like it."

I smiled, taking in everything about him in one sweeping glance. One thing was for sure; he was hardly the typical Upper East Side prep guy I was used to. There was something more to him. Something intensely masculine and unpolished in all the right ways.

"Yes, New York," I said. "Are you from here?"

"God, no," he said, gesturing for me to follow him into an office. "I don't even know how I survived the winter. I'm from North Carolina. Tar Heel born and bred."

I laughed and tugged off my scarf. I stuffed it into my purse, which I dropped onto a brown cushioned chair.

"I wouldn't get too comfortable," another voice said from the door.

I turned around and came face-to-face with a gorgeous woman with brown skin and long black hair that she wore in loose, voluminous waves.

"Moira," the woman said, holding out a hand covered in henna. "You're Lark, I presume? Toby gave me your email."

"Yes, that's me," I said, shaking Moira's hand. "Nice to meet you. Is Toby around?"

Toby was the regional campaign director for the Madison area and their boss. I'd interviewed with him twice and found him to be an eccentric, energetic man. The kind of man whose great passion would sustain us through a hard-fought campaign season. Or at least, I hoped so.

"Toby is tied up in meetings with the state team. Sam here is going to take you under his wing. He's been here nearly as long as Toby, so you're in safe hands."

"Great. I'm ready to get started."

"That's what we like to hear. At this point, you, Sam, and I are divvying up most of Madison on the ground for Governor Woodhouse. So, welcome to the team."

"It's great to finally be here."

"Thanks, Moira. I was getting to that part," Sam said with a shake of his head.

"Anytime." She turned back to me. "Are you okay with sharing this office with Sam? We're already short on space, but Josh is working on getting us the building next door."

"Yeah, that's fine by me." I snuck another glance at Sam. I caught him staring at me, and he hastily looked away when our eyes met. "Who is Josh?"

"He's Toby's immediate boss. As the state field manager, he runs the campaign for everyone in the field for the entire state of Wisconsin," Moira said. "Think of this as one big hierarchy. We work for Toby, who works for Josh, who works for the head of the Midwest organization, who works for the field campaign manager, who works for the overall campaign manager, who works for Governor Wood-house. Our job is to add to the hierarchy and get people to work underneath us. Preferably for free." She turned to the desk, grabbed two clipboards from Sam's stuff, and passed them to each of us. "Now, go bring me back seven voter registrations by five, and then we'll make a hundred phone calls."

Moira smiled cheerily and then jaunted out of the room.

I turned to Sam with wide eyes. "Is she serious?"

Sam laughed. "That's Moira for you. Come on. I'll show you the ropes."

"Just like that? I mean...I don't even get to see the office or drop my stuff at my apartment or anything?"

"Welcome to the campaign," Sam said with a wink.

I looked down at my high heels and shook my head. "At least let me find some sneakers."

His eyes traveled to my shoes, and unbidden, his laughter boomed out of him. I couldn't help it. Suddenly, I was laughing with him.

"Not my smartest move," I admitted.

"Definitely not in the snow."

I tucked the clipboard under my arm, grabbed my bag, and then headed out to the car my parents had insisted on for my time in Madison. I'd managed to keep them from buying a flashy Mercedes. They'd been appalled that I wanted a low-key Subaru but finally relented.

Of course, I hadn't told them it was because for the first time in my life, I wasn't going to be Larkin St. Vincent, but just Lark. Not an heir to an empire. Just a girl.

"Drive all the way here from New York?" Sam asked as I dug through my suitcase in the trunk.

"Oh god, no." I shot him a skeptical look. "I'm not a great driver. I didn't even get a license until I went to college."

7

"That's insane to me. I grew up driving all the back roads long before I had a license."

I pulled out my sneakers and snapped the trunk shut. I tossed Sam the keys. "By all means, Country Boy."

He laughed. "I'll show you how it's done, City Girl."

II

"You guys getting all of this?" Toby asked, bouncing from foot to foot with excitement.

I sat with Sam and Moira in the rickety plastic chairs. We glanced up at our boss and nodded encouragingly. Sam gave him a thumbs-up.

Moira leaned in and said, "We are one hundred and ten percent focused."

"Excellent. I'm ready to implement all this new knowledge and crush those numbers."

Toby held his hand up, and Moira sighed and then gave him a high five. Toby went down the row, high-fiving Sam and then finally me.

"Okay, back to the material!"

I shook my head as Toby jogged back up to the front of the room to stand with the other field managers as the presentation continued. We'd been at this state-level training at a warehouse outside of Madison all day. It was exhausting and repetitive.

I'd spent the last three weeks with Sam at the office. He'd mentored me through the basics of campaign life. I had my own assignments and tasks to complete for my section of Madison, which primarily included State Street and the University of Wisconsin–Madison. But Sam was the person I called when I had a question. He was the person who walked me through the voter registration laws, pulling call lists, entering data into the voter system, and a myriad of other things. This statewide training was a lot of the same information recycled back, and I had to admit that I'd liked hearing it from Sam first.

"Are you guys pumped up?" Moira asked with an eye roll. "Or are you snoozing?"

"So pumped up," I said dryly.

"It's not *that* bad," Sam said.

"You've been to at least three of these. Don't you ever get sick of it?" Moira asked.

"Sure. But they really do it for the newbies, like Lark."

I wrinkled my nose at him. "Hey, my teacher already covered this material. I'm pretty sure I aced the exam."

Sam chuckled and leaned back in the uncomfortable plastic chair. "I meant that it pumps up the newbs.

Gives you that extra bit of excitement to really make it through the next couple of months."

"Plus, it's the only day we get to sit around and do nothing," Moira added.

"And eat lunch, *sitting down*." Sam wiggled his fingers at me, and I laughed.

"Who knew I'd be so excited to eat lunch like a regular person? Instead of grabbing something on the go and shoving it down my throat as fast as I can."

Sam gawked, and Moira snickered.

"Phrasing," Moira said.

"Oh my god! That's not what I meant!"

"Shh," a girl hissed directly in front of us.

Sam whispered, "Sorry," to the girl and then went right back to chatting. "Anyway, where should we go for lunch?"

"What's even around here?" Moira asked, pulling her dark hair back into a bun on the top of her head with a pencil. "If we were downtown, I'd say Pel'meni."

"You always vote for Pel'meni," Sam said. He turned to face me, and I froze under that gaze. "Do you have a preference?"

I opened my mouth to respond, but then he gently brushed a strand of chestnut-red hair that had fallen loose from my ponytail behind my ear. I lost coherent thought in that second.

"Let me guess. Burgers?" he asked with his award-winning smile. His hand lingered for a second longer. "With no mustard because it's disgusting?"

I swallowed. "Yes, please."

"Burgers it is," Sam said, finally dropping his hand.

I knew that I should look away. That I should ignore the way my heart pitter-pattered in my chest. I didn't have time for these feelings. God, none of us did. I worked from nine in the morning until ten at night every single day of the week. It was hardly sustainable. Let alone adding in anything other than food and the occasional drink. Sleep was more important. I guarded it with my life. And yet, staring into those eyes, I was seriously considering forsaking sleep. Forsaking a lot of sleep.

Then Sam broke the trance, and I bit my lip to keep from sighing. I was ninety-nine percent sure it was one-sided. That was also new for me. Dates had always been easy to get and utterly mindless. But while being around Sam was easy, nothing about him was mindless.

Which was the main reason I was so attracted to him. He was good-looking. By all means, the tall, dark, and handsome thing really worked for him. But it was so much more than that. He was rugged where I was used to preps. He was passionate where I expected apathy. He was driven, motivated, and hard-working where I'd only known privilege and entitlement. His confidence wasn't born out of how much money resided in his bank account, but from the pride he took in his work. I'd never met anyone like Sam Rutherford.

"We only have a few more minutes before lunch," Josh said, drawing my attention back to him. He double-checked his watch. "You'll have an hour to eat, and then I'll need you back in your seats for the afternoon session. Everyone understand?"

The room grumbled a collective, "Yes." We were all ready to get out of there.

My eyes still darted to Sam's. To my surprise, he had just glanced over at me, too.

He smiled that disarming smile and said, "Ready for lunch?"

"Yeah," I said softly. "Lunch sounds great."

"Cool. I'm going to snag a Coke before we head out. Want one?"

"Just a water."

"Got it!"

Sam popped up and disappeared into the ensuing crowd. Lunch was only an hour, and all the campaign workers were in a hurry to make the most of their meal.

"The rest of the campaign is going to be so fun, watching you two," Moira said. Her dark eyes were filled with laughter.

"What do you mean?" I asked cautiously.

"Oh, please. You both have it bad."

"No way, Moira. Sam is a nice guy and he's mentoring me and...he's not interested."

She rolled her eyes. "And I'm a dodo bird."

I couldn't help but ask, "You think he's interested in me?"

"Does he have eyes?" Moira demanded.

"Well, it doesn't matter, does it? I'm not here for a relationship. I'm here to get Woodhouse elected."

"You're right," Moira said, throwing her arm over my shoulders as Sam appeared.

"All set?" Sam asked.

He passed me a water, and I mumbled, "Thank you."

"Oh, we're ready," Moira said. "Right, Lark?"

I tilted my chin up, refusing to back down. I liked Moira and Sam and everyone else on the campaign, but Woodhouse was the real reason that I was here. A boy was not going to get in the way of me following my dream.

"Yep. I am so ready."

III

I held the box of clipboards to my chest. I'd spent all afternoon on campus with a handful of volunteers, doing voter registration at the end-of-semester events at the University of Wisconsin.

With my hands full, I toed the door to the office open and nearly collapsed once I dropped the box onto the counter.

"God, I need to work out more." I stretched my arms and shoulders. "The walk from campus is literally killing me."

Sam strolled out of our joint office and into the main room. "We should get you a rolling cart or something."

"Please do. It'll save my poor, precious arms." I held them out in front of me and shook them like spaghetti.

Sam laughed and reached into the box of clipboards to count the voter registration forms. He whistled. "Forty-seven. What line are you feeding these undergrads?"

"No line," I said with a shrug. "I'm pretty."

Sam guffawed. "Who knew that was all you needed? I'm sure Toby will be happy tonight when we recap numbers."

"I am starving," I murmured. I glanced down at my phone. "We have twenty-three minutes until we have to make calls. Food?" I fluttered my eyelashes at him. "Please."

"Yes, food for sure. Let me drop these off for data entry, and then we can go."

"Oh, thank god."

I sank into my office chair in the space I still shared with Sam. Even though we'd gotten more space and Toby had said I could have my own office, I'd just gotten used to sharing. Plus, I had to admit that I liked being close to Sam.

I picked up my purse and responded to a few texts as I waited for Sam to return. I yawned dramatically and barely managed to cover it with my hand. I'd gone out with Sam and Moira for drinks last night, and I was so fucking tired. I'd been tired all day. I'd really needed that drink last night, but damn, I missed that extra hour of sleep.

"Okay, all set," Sam said.

"Great!" I said and followed him out of the office.

We wandered across the street and into our favorite burger place near the square. The capitol building stood on the hill, overlooking the rest of the city. It was beautiful and a smaller replica of the capitol in DC. I appreciated that I could see it from anywhere on State Street.

We ordered our burgers and took our meals back to our booth in the corner. We came over nearly every afternoon. Sometimes, he just liked to have his mentoring time there instead of being cooped up in the office with everyone else. It was one-on-one time.

"Did I tell you about Kristy?" Sam asked once we sat down.

"Kristy? Like, volunteer-housing Kristy?"

Like most people on the campaign, Sam had been placed in a volunteers' home for the season. He'd been living in Kristy's extra room in the basement for months. But I knew that he'd been looking to get his own place.

"Yeah. I guess her daughter graduated this semester and is moving back home. So, now, I have to find somewhere else to live."

"When do you have to leave?"

"Tomorrow."

My mouth dropped. "Do you have another volunteer's home lined up? Or did you find a place of your own?"

"Toby is calling the other volunteers who offered to

house a staff member, but right now, it looks like I'm sleeping on Toby's floor or getting a hotel until we figure it out. I'm going to go through all the listings for houses. I have enough saved for a down payment."

"That's awful. I hate that it happened so fast."

"Yeah. The living situation is my least favorite part of all of this."

I bit my lip. Did I dare say what was on my mind?

"Well...you know, I have a pull-out couch in my apartment," I said, staring down at my food. "You could stay with me for a while. You know...until you find your own place."

"Oh, well, I'm trying to avoid paying rent," he said with a laugh.

"Actually, my parents pay for it." I took a huge bite of my burger to keep from saying anything more.

My parents had flat-out bought the condo on the top floor of one of the buildings in downtown Madison. They were the controlling type, and money was never an issue. So, they'd simply looked for the nicest place they could find and purchased it. The only say I'd even had in the matter was to convince them to get as close to the office as possible. They'd relented.

Not that I planned to tell Sam any of that. He didn't know who I was or what my parents did or that I came from money. And I liked it that way. He treated me just like everyone else. Everyone on campaign did.

"Are you okay with me crashing on your couch? I

mean, I don't know if you like your space to decompress after work," he said carefully. His brown eyes said something else though. "It would just be temporary."

And I really hoped I wasn't misreading that look. I hoped that Moira was right and Sam really did like me. Because the last few weeks had been torture.

"I don't mind. And anyway, there's no reason for you to sleep on the floor or get a hotel when I have a perfectly fine substitute. At least until you find your own place."

He grinned, and it made me squirm. Why did he have to be so attractive? And so different than every other guy I'd ever met?

"All right. Well, I'll pile everything into the truck and come over after work."

"I can help if you need it."

"You're already a big help."

I tried to hide my pleased grin.

Sam was moving in with me. I probably shouldn't have offered. It would put us in close quarters, even more than we were at the office. I was tempting fate by having him in my apartment. But I couldn't help but tempt fate with him.

IV

It was after ten when we were finally done packing up Sam's belongings and putting them in his truck. I took one look at that truck and laughed. Every time I saw the beaten-up old Chevy, I couldn't keep it together. I was interested in a man who drove an old truck. My parents would probably disown me on principle.

"You ready?" Sam asked, stowing his last box.

"Yeah."

"Were you laughing at my truck again?"

I couldn't help but laugh again. "I'm not used to it."

"Maybe you should drive her." He offered me the keys.

I quickly backed away. "Oh, dear god, no. I'll wreck it, and then you'll be without a home or a car. And I'll ruin all your things in the accident. We'd better not."

"One day, I'll get you to drive my truck."

"No way." I shook my head. "That's not happening."

He chuckled and then hopped into the driver's seat. I followed him across town in my Subaru, which had most of his clothes in it. Then, we spent the next half hour unloading all of his stuff into a corner of the apartment. I was hyper-cognizant of the quality of the apartment. Like it was a ticking time bomb, and any second, it would explode, and he'd know all of my carefully kept secrets.

"This is really nice, Lark," Sam said.

"Thanks," I said softly, biting down on my lip.

He peeked into the open door of my bedroom. It was a massive master suite with enough space for two beds, a walk-in closet that could have been a second room, and a bathroom that I was glad he couldn't see at first glance with its giant waterfall shower and a free-standing jetted tub.

"Damn! This place is crazy. A little surprised it's only one-bedroom."

My parents had wanted a two-bedroom, had insisted on it actually, until they'd found this floor plan.

I shrugged off his comment. "Two bedrooms would probably be better for you right about now."

He laughed. "Maybe. Well, thank you for letting me stay."

"Anytime."

He grinned, and my heart melted.

"I should probably take a quick shower. Carrying all those boxes was quite a workout."

My heart deflated. Right. A shower. There was only one bathroom. So, I'd have to show him that.

I swallowed. "Sure. The shower is the first door on the right. Help yourself to anything you need. I am going to have some ice cream. Want any?"

"What do you have?"

"Pretty much everything, except strawberry," I told him. "I'm allergic."

"Good to know. I'll take whatever you're having. I'll just be a minute."

I nodded and watched him retreat into the bathroom, worrying at my lip with my top teeth. It would be fine. Or at least, I tried to convince myself of that.

To distract myself, I pulled out a container of chocolate chip cookie dough and rocky road and then combined them with a chocolate drizzle on top. I never had time to go to the grocery store, but I always had time for ice cream.

True to his word, Sam appeared back in the living room in less than ten minutes, freshly showered and dressed in basketball shorts and a gray T-shirt. My eyes snagged on his biceps and went down, down, down. And then way back up.

Color hit my cheeks, and I pushed a bowl into his hands. "Here you go."

"Your shower is pretty epic," he said, sinking into the couch next to me.

"Uh, yeah. Thanks. I was not expecting that," I lied. "Really nice, huh?"

"Yeah. Looks like the showers I installed in the rich houses I built with my dad back home."

"Oh, yeah?" I had known that Sam worked construction with his father, but I hadn't known what kind of work he'd done.

"Yeah, this place is a really great find. Your parents chose well."

My cheeks heated, and I hastily pulled up Netflix. I'd fallen asleep on the couch the night before in the middle of an episode of *Parks and Recreation*, and it picked up where I'd left off.

"The campaign episodes?" Sam said, shifting the topic away from my apartment. I nearly sighed with relief. "Those are my favorite."

"Ben and Leslie are perfect for each other."

"Yeah, but Aubrey Plaza."

"I know, right?" I said with a laugh. "April always says everything I think."

"No way are you that dark."

"You have no idea," I said, wiggling my eyebrows.

"Nah, you're like the sweet girl from the city."

I laughed, setting my ice cream on the coffee table. He couldn't be further from the truth. "There are no

23

sweet city girls, Sam. That's something you just invented."

Sam reached out and pushed a strand of my hair behind my ear. Our eyes locked, and I swore I stopped breathing. His hand trailed over the shell of my ear and then to my neck. The softest touch, as if he knew that he should stop but he didn't.

"You don't give yourself enough credit."

I swallowed. "You give me too much."

"Well, whatever we might have been before, we're here now, in the same place, doing the same thing. I think that's all that matters."

"Yeah," I whispered in agreement.

We didn't break eye contact. He was still touching me. My heart hammered in my chest. We were so close and yet so far. And I didn't know if I should cross that line. All the logical reasons floated out of my brain. Logic and reason were secondary to matters of the heart.

We moved as one, as if pulled by a string. Magnets seeking out the other. My hands pushed into his hair. His grasped my waist, tugging me tight against him. Our lips hovered an inch away and then crashed together. As if the weeks we'd spent in that small office and days of working together and hours of mentoring and every minute and second in each other's presence had coalesced into this moment.

Our lips moved together. Hands roamed. Tongues

met. Fire and tension and rapture exploded all around us. Every kiss before this was muted and then utterly disappeared. There was no kiss before this. There was nothing before this.

Just me and Sam.

Two bodies.

One heart.

Then, we slowed and stopped and looked on in a state of euphoria and wonder.

"I've wanted to do that since the first time I saw you," Sam said breathlessly.

His hands had somehow become tangled in my hair. I was practically sitting in his lap.

"Me too."

I kissed him again—thoroughly.

"We should probably stop."

"Uh-huh," I said against his lips.

"Or not," he said and then kissed me some more.

And then some more.

Heedless of our different backgrounds or what lay ahead, we didn't stop kissing until long into the night when I fell soundly asleep on the couch, wrapped in Sam's arms.

SPRING

I

If I'd had a two-bedroom apartment, Sam would have moved in with me.

I wanted him to. As irrational as that was. Here I was with a secret identity, and I wanted to bring a stranger into my safe haven. It was close enough that he'd been *to* my apartment, let alone stayed there for the week before he could get his own place.

It was worse when he left.

Because I didn't want him to. And I was pretty sure that I'd never cared this much about anyone. I never wanted anyone to stay.

It wasn't the way I had been raised. The Upper East Side was its own version of fucked up. I'd grown up with controlling parents, four crazy best friends, and too much money. I'd gotten everything I ever wanted and never had any boundaries...except to fall in line with the family.

I'd been raised to follow my family's footsteps. I'd gotten my bachelor's from Brown and a JD from Columbia, and I was supposed to magically take over St. Vincent's Enterprise. Until I'd seen Governor Woodhouse speak in the city, and it had changed everything. He was a man I could get behind. A person I believed in. And I suddenly didn't want to follow the perfect trajectory. I wanted to make a difference.

Which was how I'd ended up here with a one-year term from my parents before I came home and took over my legacy. I intended to make the most of it.

But none of that would make a difference if Wood-house wasn't nominated for the presidency. He was the front-runner after winning the New Hampshire primary and a spatter of other early states. Wisconsin's primary race was right around the corner, and the campaign was laser-focused on it.

I had planned a vote-athon at the university for the day that early vote opened up. A twenty-four-hour dance party inside the Union ballroom. It would end the next morning with everyone walking from the party to the polling place on campus.

Fifteen hours into it at midnight, I could barely keep my eyes open. The students were really in charge of it all. I'd gotten the student party association to host the event so that we could have it on campus. The campaign hours left me so run-down that pulling an all-nighter sounded like a nightmare, which I hadn't considered when I suggested the event.

"You look like you could use this," Sam said.

I desperately reached out for the coffee. "You are a lifesaver."

He laughed. "I don't want you to pass out. Sleep is our greatest ally. Forgoing it for a night does not seem like your best idea."

I took a long sip of the steaming hot black coffee. "It really isn't. But I'm here now. I can power through until morning."

"That's seven more hours, and you look dead on your feet. Maybe you should get a few hours of shut-eye while your volunteers handle this."

"Don't be reasonable," I said with a grin.

"Just looking out for you."

I waved my hand. "I know. I know. But this is my first big event. I don't feel comfortable walking away, even for a few hours."

"I was afraid you were going to say that," he said, swiping a hand back through his dark hair. My eyes followed the motion with keen interest. "I'm going to have to stay up with you."

"What?" I asked with a laugh. "Don't be silly. You need your sleep."

"You think I'm going to let you early vote before me?"

I rolled my eyes. "They all count the same."

He stepped forward, closer and closer. My heart rate picked up. He was so close and yet so far. We'd kissed a few more times since that first night, but we hadn't decided on anything. We hadn't confirmed anything. This felt like another step. An unknowable step for us.

Slowly, his pinkie slid around my own pinkie. A small, simple motion, and still, electricity zinged through my body. Everything jolted as if he'd zapped me awake for the first time.

We stayed like that for I didn't know how long, watching the night blur on. All the college students moved along to made-up choreography that they planned to dance on their way to the polls. We even joined in with some of them to keep ourselves awake.

We grabbed burgers from our favorite burger joint, which I'd convinced to donate to the event. With only a matter of hours before we could get out of here, Sam and I sank onto the floor of the ballroom and ate our favorite food.

"Lark," Sam said when he finally finished.

I took my last bite of my burger and set the wrapper aside. After I finished chewing, I asked, "Yeah?"

"You don't mind me being here, do you?"

My cheeks flushed. "Mind? No. I...I want you here."

He nodded. "Good. I don't want to step over any boundaries. I know that we're coworkers..."

I put my hand on his. "You're not overstepping."

If anything, he was going slow. So, so *slow*. I wasn't used to guys like Sam. Southern gentlemen who cared whether or not they were going too fast or overstepping. Guys who wanted more than sex from me. We'd been circling each other for weeks and not done more than kiss. To think that he'd thought that was overstepping, I never even would have guessed.

"I just...I really like you," he admitted.

A smile came to my face. "I really like you, too."

I leaned forward then, capturing his lips against mine. It was gentle. None of the hurried rush that I was used to from guys. This was the settling of what had already been brewing between us. The rightness of it sliding into place.

He groaned against my lips and pulled back. "You make it really hard to not just pick you up and steal you."

I chuckled, drawing him in again. "Who said I wouldn't want that?"

He kissed me one more time. "You're too special for that," he said against my lips. "You don't rush perfection, Lark. And I don't want to rush us."

"Us," I breathed the word like a lifeline.

"You are mine, right?" he asked.

I swallowed and nodded, meeting those deep, dark eyes. "I am."

"Good." He tucked a lock of red hair behind my ear. "I feel like I've been waiting forever for you."

"You do?" I whispered in awe. No one had ever talked about me like that.

His smile made his eyes crinkle. It was the most genuine smile I'd ever seen from anyone in my entire life. Sam was one of a kind.

"I'm glad the wait is over."

II

"To Governor Woodhouse! The winner of the Wisconsin primary and presumptive winner of the presidential primary!" Moira cried, holding her beer aloft.

We all lifted our glasses to meet hers and cheered our victory. The primary had been grueling, but now that it was behind us, the future looked even brighter. There had always been the chance that Woodhouse wouldn't be nominated, and then we'd all have to close up shop and hop to another candidate. Or more likely, in my case, head back home.

"God, I love this place," Sam said as a platter of fries were set out before us.

We were currently inside The Station, our favorite bar in town—primarily because it also served after-hours bar grub. Not the best place to eat in town, but they served beer, too. So, win-win.

I reached for the fries, dunking them in ketchup and wrinkling my nose as Moira went for the mustard. "I don't know how you can stand that stuff."

"Well, I don't know how you can be allergic to strawberries. Do you know how good they are?" Moira asked.

I shook my head. "As if I have a choice in what I'm allergic to."

Moira shrugged. "If you say so."

"Says the woman with more allergies than anyone I've met."

"But yeah, I'm just allergic to grass and trees and rabbits and, like, most of nature. Not wonderful, delicious foods, like strawberries."

"You have such an interesting view on this," Sam said.

"Hey now," Moira said, pointing at him. "I don't need the boyfriend to gang up on me."

A flush moved up my neck and into my cheeks. I still wasn't used to that word out of anyone's mouth. Sam *was* my boyfriend. And I was his girlfriend. It felt surreal and like it was absolutely perfect. No wonder I'd never really had a serious boyfriend before this. Just lots and lots of casual dates.

Sam stuffed another fry in his mouth. "Don't get mad at us because you're pining over Toby."

"Whoa!" Moira said, holding up her hands. "I am not *pining* for Toby."

I snort-laughed. "Yes, you are."

"That is outrageous."

"We all know it, Moira," Sam said with a shrug.

Moira looked on indignantly. "I do not pine. I can have whoever I want. And I'll have you know that I left an ex back home, pining after me. Might hook back up with him when this is all over."

Sam laughed. "Whatever you want us to think."

Moira stood from her seat and rolled her eyes. "I'm going to the other table where they appreciate me."

I reached for Moira's hand. "Come on. Don't be like that."

She winked at me with her own giggle and then wandered to the other table of campaign workers from our state office.

"She's so touchy sometimes," Sam said.

"She's Moira. I love her."

He nodded. "She's the best." He finished off the fries and dove into the basket of wings. "What about you?"

"What about me?" I asked as I reached for a barbecue one.

"Do you have someone waiting for you back in New York?"

"Oh," I said, biting my lip. "No. I don't have anyone."

"Really? No exes?"

I shrugged. "I mean, I dated people, but I was never serious."

Sam looked at me like he wanted me to continue. He was eating a wing and patiently waiting for me to say more. Which was...fuck. Okay, I'd have to say more. But what could I say that wouldn't incriminate myself?

"My parents are kind of controlling," I told him evenly. "Weirdly controlling about some things...like my career path. And also, somehow, very flippant about most other things. They don't care who I date or really anything I do as long as I stay on the right trajectory."

"That sounds freeing and also constricting."

"Exactly," I said, relieved that I could get him to understand without revealing everything. I wasn't ready for that yet. "So, I did a lot of, uh...uh, rebellious things in high school and college to try to find the boundaries that were never there."

"Ah," he said, as if catching on. "So, no boyfriends but lots of...dating."

"Yeah. The only people I ever really had in my life were my crew."

He raised an eyebrow in question.

"I grew up with four best friends—Penn, Katherine, Lewis, and Rowe. We have a fraught history, but we've always been there for each other."

"That sounds nice," he said. "I've always been like that with my brother, Jake."

"I'm an only child. So, my family is the crew."

I glanced down at my plate. I didn't exactly want to tell him that I'd fooled around a lot, growing up. That pushing those boundaries meant pushing them with everyone, including my friends. That I'd actually slept with Penn, Lewis, and Rowe at some point. That I wasn't this person. This *good girl* he knew was an illusion. I'd always been something...someone else. I liked the person he saw. The normal girl he was falling for.

"At least you have them," he said.

I nodded. "Otherwise, this might be the first time I've ever been serious about anyone."

When I looked back up at him, he was smiling broad. "Really? I like being your first."

I swallowed as I felt myself sink deeper into Sam. I wasn't lying about my past. Not really. Just not telling all of the truth. I wasn't ready to see his reaction about who I really was. I'd seen it over and over again. The thought of Sam looking at me differently made me want to be sick. No, I couldn't tell him. Not yet.

"What about you?" I asked hastily instead. "Do you have exes?"

"Ex," he clarified. "Just one."

"Oh?" I asked, my interest piqued.

"Melissa Young," he said with a sigh. "We dated through most of college. She still lives in Chapel Hill and goes to church with my family. It's been complicated since we broke up."

"Complicated how?"

He scratched the back of his head. "I don't know. My parents want us to get back together. They like that she's a local girl. But I knew that I was leaving for over a year on campaign. I knew we'd never survive long distance."

"Why?"

"I don't know. She's...needy." He sighed heavily. "I hate saying that. She's a nice girl, and we were together for a long time." He looked deep into my eyes. "But I think if she was that easy to leave, then she wasn't ever going to be my endgame."

I considered his honesty. Hated that I couldn't reciprocate it. And found a twinge of jealousy creep up in me. That he'd had a relationship like that in the past. That his family still wanted that. If they knew who I was, I was certain they wouldn't approve. Or they'd only approve for my money...if they were that sort of people. I hoped not.

I didn't want to feel jealous. It wasn't like Melissa was here. Sam had left her before we ever met. But somehow...that Upper East Side girl inside of me couldn't hold back the petty.

I dispelled the thought. I didn't need to feel that.

After all, I was the one here with Sam.

III

"Thank you so much, Kennedy," I said to my lead volunteer.

We were enjoying an ice cream cone from the university Dairy Store on Lake Mendota. Kennedy had agreed to take charge of the event after working with me on the vote-athon.

"You really don't have to thank me, Lark," she said. "I'm so happy that we have a presence for Governor Woodhouse on campus. Four years ago, I wasn't old enough to vote, and I wanted to so badly. But so many of my classmates don't seem to get how important it is. Like they don't think politics affects them. As if taxes and student loans and tuition aren't decided by the government." She rolled her eyes.

"Well, I agree with you. I'm here after all."

"And thank god," she crooned. "We could have had anyone."

I laughed. "Anyone would have done a good job."

"But you're the best," Kennedy said as if it were a fact.

Then, she waved at another girl nearby and nodded her head to say she was going to go talk to her. I let her go. This was why *she* was here after all. Because Kennedy knew everyone. Which was how she had doubled our volunteers in the time we'd been working together. I was going to miss her over the summer when everyone cleared out of the university.

My phone buzzed in my pocket, and I reached for it, expecting to see a cute message from Sam. We'd been texting back and forth like crazy. I kept wanting to invite him over to my place after we'd had another late night at The Station. But I couldn't bring myself to do it. New York Lark would have done it, but this Lark was waiting for him to make the first move. And I knew he wanted to wait. I just didn't know what he was waiting *for*.

When I glanced down at my phone though, it wasn't from Sam at all. The screen was lit up with one word—*Mother*.

I groaned. Great. This was going to be...fantastic.

With a heavy sigh, I answered, "Mother, what a surprise."

"Hello, Larkin, darling. How is my lovely daughter?"

"I'm doing well," I said evenly. I knew she wasn't calling to hear about the campaign. She wouldn't want details. This had to be about something else. Something I was certain I didn't want to hear. "Can I help you?"

"Now, why would you think that I needed help with something?"

I looked skyward. Games. So many games. I'd almost forgotten how exhausting it was to play them. I hadn't heard from my mother since the day I moved away, set on forging my own path on the campaign trail for the next year. And now, here she was, determined to make my life more frustrating. It wasn't enough that I was working ninety-plus-hour weeks and barely sleeping. No, I had to now deal with my mother as well.

"I didn't expect to hear from you, is all," I told her bluntly. My mother hated bluntness.

"Larkin, you know what it's like. Your father is swamped with the resorts. I'm busy designing the latest line of handbags. We're both running billion-dollar companies." Her mother sighed dramatically. "We could use the help."

Oh god, here it was. The real reason for the call.

"You could come home."

I cringed. "We agreed on a year."

"Your candidate has won the primary. He probably doesn't need your help to get elected now. He's a shoo-in."

That was so far from the truth that it physically pained me. Not that my mother would care. "I can't abandon my position. This is where I'm needed until November."

"Are you really though?" my mother asked. "Needed?"

"Yes," I ground out.

"I know that you think you are, dear. But it's not true. Anyone could take your place on that campaign, and the outcome would always be the same. You're a hamster on a wheel in a giant machine there." My mother didn't sound emotional. It was all rehearsed. A robot. "You can make a difference *here*. Can't you see about what's really important, Larkin? You were raised to take over this company. *This* is where you're needed."

Something cracked inside of me at her words. My hands started shaking. My throat closed up. Tears pricked at my eyes. This wasn't supposed to happen. I was supposed to have a year. A full year without more of the same from my parents. A year free from their expectations and shoving the company down my throat. The fucking company. That was the only thing they cared about. Not me. Not their only daughter.

I couldn't breathe. I couldn't think. Everything felt

far away and deathly quiet. As if I'd entered a wind tunnel.

Whatever else my mother said was lost to me. Not that it mattered. I wasn't coming home. We'd agreed on a year. I was going to get my year.

But I couldn't push back the rising panic. I knew it was irrational. This was my mother. This was how she was. She ruled with a heavy hand and didn't so much guide as force people into the shape she wanted. This was nothing new.

None of that mattered. Not as the panic attack took over my body. I didn't know if it was the lack of sleep, the long hours, the constant pressure to perform. Or having to hide a piece of who I was at all times. Or if it was a combination of it all, but it hit me like a two-by-four to the chest.

I hung up on my mother. I didn't even remember doing it. But I couldn't get air in. I was sitting in the grass on the quad, overlooking the lake, hyperventilating. Air all around me...and none of it was in my lungs.

I squeezed my eyes shut and willed myself to stop. But it was a waste. It wasn't stopping. It wasn't going away.

I needed...I needed Sam.

Without another thought, I sent one quick text to him.

Panic attack. Help.

I couldn't see his response through my tears, but suddenly, he was there. His strong arms around my shoulders. His fingers brushing the tears off of my cheeks. His soothing words echoing in my ears. Then without a backward glance, he lifted me into his arms and carried me to his pickup truck.

I had no memory of the drive to my apartment. Just him pulling up in front of the building and rushing around to my side of the truck.

"Wait"—I hiccupped—"I have...to go back to work."

He shook his head, easing me out of the truck. "I don't think so. I think you're going to go upstairs and sleep. You need more sleep, Lark."

"But Toby..."

"Let me worry about Toby," he said more forcefully than I'd ever heard him.

I'd been wrong about Sam. I'd thought that he was quiet and soft and principled. But when I needed him, I realized that he was so much more. Commanding and authoritative. Protective and capable and caring. He could take charge with ease, and I felt...safe in his arms. I knew that he wouldn't let me down.

We made it up to my apartment, and he found clothes for me to change into. Then, he carefully eased me into bed. My tears had stopped sometime earlier, but I still felt a growing sense of panic. A panic that I couldn't erase.

"Sam," I said, reaching my hand out for him. He took it in his and kissed it. "Can you stay for a minute?"

He nodded, kicking off his boots and crawling into bed after me. He wrapped his arms around my waist and held me to him. He was silent for a minute before asking, "What happened?"

I shook my head. I didn't know how to explain. I couldn't tell him about my mother. Not like this. He knew that she was controlling, but he'd never understand why she wanted me to give this all up to take over the family company. And it was more than that. It was the two decades of pressure to perform weighing on my shoulders. The knowledge that I'd have to go back after this was over and fit back into the perfect role of Larkin St. Vincent again. When I was finally getting comfortable with just being Lark.

And damn it, this campaign was important to me! I wasn't ready to leave. Even with the shit hours and my shit sleep schedule and my shit eating schedule and everything else that I hated about the job, I still *loved* the job.

I swallowed. "It all came to a head at once. I talked to my mother, and it went...poorly. And work." I shook my head, brushing at another tear. "My brain couldn't keep up. I'm broken."

Sam squeezed me tighter to him. "You're not broken. You're just stressed. We all are. You need more sleep."

"I'd sleep better with you here," I whispered baldly into the silence.

He chuckled against my shoulder and then placed a kiss there. "Well, maybe we can arrange that here soon."

I shivered at the implication and heat in his voice. "I'd like that."

He kissed my neck. "But right now, sleep," he whispered against my skin. "You can relax. I'll be here for you. Right here for you always."

SUMMER

I

"Do you have everything?" Sam asked from where he was sprawled on my bed.

"You haven't told me where we're going. How do I know if I have everything?"

"We have our first day off since Christmas, Lark. Who cares where we're going?"

When Toby had confirmed that we'd finally get a much-needed day off, Sam had immediately stepped into action, telling me that he was going to steal me and to not make any plans. True to my word, no plans. I'd let him do everything.

"How much more stuff do you need for one day?" he grumbled.

"A lot," I said.

I grinned at him and then threw in the only little lacy bit I'd brought with me from home. My hopes were up that we were going to finally seal the deal now that we were going away. We'd been fooling around for a while. Done everything but sex, and I was *ready*. More than ready. He'd said he didn't want to rush us, but we were past the point of being rushed. It was *time*.

I closed my suitcase and then wheeled it out to him. "Okay, now, I'm ready."

"Excellent."

He hopped off of the bed and wrapped his arms around me, pinning me back against the closet door. His lips were hot on mine. I wanted this and so much more. So fucking much more.

My fingers drifted to the button of his jeans. I flicked it open, and he laughed gruffly against me.

"Now, now…"

I groaned. "Sam…"

"We have a drive ahead of us. We should get going if we want to get there at a decent hour."

"What if I want to keep you and stay here?" I suggested.

He kissed me again thoroughly. "Humor me."

I nodded my head with a small sigh. "All right. Will you tell me where we're going then?"

He grabbed my suitcase and then headed for the door.

"Sam?" I begged, following behind.

He winked at me. "Chicago."

I grinned like a fool. "Really?"

"Yeah, really. Now, get your ass in the car, so we can go."

I did as he'd said, sliding into the passenger seat of my Subaru. The drive was about two and a half hours, and by the time we made it to our hotel, it was late. I was already tired from the exhausting couple of weeks, but the drive had made me sleepy, too. I shook it off as we parked in the garage. He grabbed his duffel and then wheeled my suitcase inside the Palmer House.

I nearly sighed with relief. I hadn't known how much I'd missed a real city until I was back in one. Chicago wasn't New York, but it was better than nothing.

Plus, even I could admit that the Palmer House was a gorgeous hotel. An enormous, high-painted ceiling with columns bracketing the lobby and large red-carpeted staircases. If we weren't staying at a Percy hotel, this was a good option.

Sam quickly checked in and then came back to me. I bit my lip, debating on what I was about to do and then decided it was do or die. Might as well make the most of it.

"I got you an extra key," he said, passing it to me.

"Thanks. You know, let me talk to them. I bet I can get an upgrade."

He laughed. "You think?"

"I'm really good at it."

He handed me the rest of the information and his ID. "If you want to try."

"Be right back."

I walked up to the counter and smiled at the man behind the desk.

"Can I help you?" he asked.

"Hi, I'm Larkin St. Vincent," I said, sliding him my black card. "Upgrade us to the penthouse."

His eyes widened at that name. Even here, my family made waves. "Of...of course, Miss St. Vincent."

Another minute later, and I had the keys to the top floor. I dragged Sam to the private elevator that took us up, up, up, and then we burst into our suite. His eyes rounded in shock.

"You talked your way into *this*?" he asked incredulously. "What the hell did you tell them?"

I carefully shut the door behind me and headed into our living quarters. I didn't know what room Sam had reserved, but this had three bedrooms, a living room, dining room, pool table, Jacuzzi, and the best view of the city imaginable. It was exactly the sort of room that Larkin St. Vincent would get. Just not the Lark that Sam had gotten to know. I didn't know which me was me. But I knew that if I wanted to be with him, I couldn't keep hiding who I was any longer.

"I have something to tell you," I said, turning to face him.

He'd stripped out of his winter jacket and looked at

me with confusion. "That sounds serious."

"It is...a bit," I admitted.

"Okay. Should I sit down?"

I shook my head. "I've been hiding part of who I am. I told you that I'm Lark Vincent, but that's not exactly true." I waved my hand. "Well, it is, and it isn't."

"I don't understand."

"Larkin St. Vincent," I blurted out. "Of St. Vincent's Resorts and St. Vincent's handbags and cosmetics." I swallowed. "I'm the sole heir to St. Vincent's Enterprise."

Sam sank into the chair with a plop. "Oh."

I bit my lip and looked away. I hated that *oh*. I knew what it meant. I'd seen it in people all my life. Heat colored my cheeks. Shit. I'd thought that it would be different with Sam. I'd thought that telling him wouldn't change anything. Or at least, I'd hoped it wouldn't. That it would be different than everyone else in my life. For so long, people had seen me as dollar signs or a name. It was exhausting.

"Yeah," I said softly, crossing my arms over my chest. "I guess...this is why I don't tell anyone."

"Why is that?" he asked.

"Because they look at me like that." I pointed at him.

"How am I looking at you?"

I shrugged.

He came to stand before me and tipped my chin

up. "How am I looking at you?"

But when I stared deep into his dark depths, it wasn't there. I wasn't just my parents' money in his eyes.

"Usually, people get weird about it," I admitted. "They start to see me for something else."

"Lark, I only see you for you. Who your parents are, how much money you have, whether or not you're an heiress," he said with a soft laugh, "none of that matters to me."

I swallowed. "Really?"

He nodded. "In fact, I hate that you ever had to lie about your identity. Though I think it all makes sense now."

"What does?"

"I've been taking things slow with you because I felt like that was what you wanted. Like...you were hiding yourself from me. You weren't fully into this."

"I was. I *am*," I gasped.

He stroked my cheek with his thumb. "I know. I see that now. I think I thought that you pulling back from me had something to do with our relationship. But I was seeing your fear about revealing who you really are."

"I'm sorry," I told him. "I hated hiding. I just wanted to be...normal."

He chuckled and kissed me hard once. "Normal is overrated."

II

"Sam, please," I whispered against his lips.

I pushed my fingers up into his hair, trying to get more of him. More, more, more. I couldn't get enough.

He didn't try to stop me or slow us down. He leaned into my kiss, sliding his tongue along the seam of my lips and opening me to him. Our kiss deepened, intensified, until I felt like I could barely breathe. I wanted him to devour me whole.

He seemed to sense that in my mood. The next thing I knew, he reached down and hoisted my legs up and around his hips. I gasped, wrapping my arms around his neck and securing myself to him. But he was already walking us toward the open bedroom door.

My back hit one of the posters, and he ground

against me. I whimpered in desperation. Fuck, I wanted him. I wanted him so bad. Waiting had been so hard. But he'd known something was off even though I'd never told him. Sam *knew* me. Better than my parents. Better than anyone maybe. He'd seen the truth. He just hadn't known what it was.

And I loved him for it.

The thought shook me to my core. I'd fallen in love with him.

This was what it was supposed to feel like.

Not the sham of relationships I'd had growing up. Not the thing they said it was, but what it *really* was. The highest high. Like I was soaring above the clouds. Everything in the world disappeared. And together, we transcended time, space, and reality. Until there was just this moment. I was perfectly okay with that. I was perfectly okay with falling in love with Sam Rutherford.

But I was done waiting. We were stronger, happier for it, but it didn't mean that I wanted to wait a second longer now that we were on the same page.

"God, Lark, I've wanted this for so long," he said, breaking from me and lowering me to my feet.

"Me too. So much."

He stripped me from my jeans with practiced ease. My sweater came next along with the tank top I wore under it in lieu of a bra. I stood before him in nothing but a thong, and soon, that was gone, too.

We'd gotten here before. Done everything but sex. And I trembled with need at the knowledge that there would be no stopping, no complaints about getting sleep or having to work the next day. Just us together. Like I wanted.

Sam dropped to his knees before me, lifting one leg over his shoulder. He slid his hand up my inner thigh until he brushed against my core. I jerked slightly at his touch, but soon, his mouth replaced his fingers.

"Oh fuck," I groaned at the first flick of his tongue against my clit.

I reached up and grasped the poster on the bed to hold myself in place. I felt like any second I was going to collapse as he pleasured me with his skilled tongue. A second later, he inserted a finger inside of me, and my moans were audible. A second finger followed, and I half-wanted to ride him I was so turned on. My orgasm hit me in a rocking spasm all at once. It was like the two-and-a-half-hour ride up to Chicago had been all the foreplay I needed.

"Fuck, Lark," he said.

His eyes were glazed with need as he rose to his feet and removed his own clothing.

"I want you," I told him.

He grinned a cocky smile that I claimed as my own. I'd only ever seen him use that particular smile with me. And I was perfectly okay with that.

My eyes rounded at the sight of him as he stripped

out of his boxers. He jutted upward, hard as a rock. As if my own climax had made him as hot as it had made me. I reached out and took the length of him in my hand. I experimentally pumped up and down, up and down. He twitched in my hand, clearly enjoying my ministrations.

"Lark," he groaned.

"Should I taste you?"

He clutched my arms and pushed me back a step closer to the bed. "I've waited for you this long. I'm not waiting any longer."

My smile was teasing. "How do you want me?"

He withdrew a condom and placed it in my hand.

I tore the foil and removed the condom. "Tell me."

He chuckled softly. "You're issuing commands now?"

I stroked his dick one more time and then pressed the condom to the head of him, ever so slowly dragging it down his length. "I like to know."

"I want to get inside of you, Lark," he told me. "I want to make love to you."

Make love.

My heart stuttered in my chest.

Not fuck.

Not have sex.

He wanted to *make love* to me.

"You do?" I whispered, losing my bravado.

His eyes were bright with need when he looked down at me. "Yes. I love you, Lark."

I inhaled sharply at the words. The words I'd thought but hadn't been able to say aloud. It was as if he'd read my mind. Seen deep inside of me and known my soul. It amazed me that we were on the same page. Thinking the same thing in nearly the same moment.

"I love you, too," I whispered back.

Something I'd never told another person. Not once. And I was glad because they never would have been true before this.

I crawled backward on the bed, and Sam followed me, laying his weight across me. Our eyes caught and held. I loved him. It was a surreal moment. And it felt utterly, perfectly, unanimously right. That we had always been leading up to this moment. From that first day on the campaign when I'd walked into the office.

He brushed a lock of my red hair out of my face and then eased forward into me. I was already so primed that there was no resistance. He slid in like he was always meant to be there. My missing puzzle piece.

Our bodies moved together. A fluid motion so smooth and familiar, it was as if we'd done this before. And I didn't want to stop. Not as he brought his lips onto mine. Not as I snaked my legs around his waist to draw him closer against me. Not as his hands dug into my hips so that he could drive into me faster. Not when we hit the peak and fell off together.

Stars exploded in my vision as I cried out into the night. He was right there with me.

My body turned to mush. Sweat coated my pale, freckled skin. My chest heaved up and down from the exertion.

And I felt the best I'd ever felt.

"Please tell me that you brought more condoms," I said in between deep breaths.

Sam laughed and kissed my shoulder before sliding out of me and heading for the bathroom. "You're in luck, City Girl."

I chuckled and threw my hands above my head in delight. Exhaustion took me just as hard, and by the time he returned, I was nearly asleep. I never slept enough on campaign. It was hard to calm down after such crazy days and harder to wake up. To feel this relaxed was almost unheard of.

"Going to fall asleep on me already?" Sam asked, running a hand down my back.

"So comfortable."

"I have a present for you."

I rolled over and groggily opened my eyes. "A present?"

He nodded. Then he held out a carefully wrapped gift.

I grabbed my sweater off the end of the bed and pulled it on over my head before reaching for the package, which was about the size of my palm. I slowly unwrapped it. My hand went to my mouth as I realized what I was looking at. Nestled in the center of the paper was a small wooden lark.

"Is this...me?" I asked. My eyes lifted to his. "Did you make this?"

He sank onto the bed next to me. "Yeah. My dad taught me to carve when I was young. It's a hobby that soothes me when I can't get my brain to shut off. So, I've been working on it for a couple months right before bed."

I pulled the bird to my chest. "Sam, thank you. This means so much."

"I know it's not what you're used to," he said after a minute.

I shook my head. "No, don't condition it. It's perfect."

"I'm glad you like it," he said and softly kissed me again. "And I'm glad that you told me who you are. That must have been difficult."

"No, I never should have hidden from you in the first place."

"I understand why you did. You didn't want to be judged for who you are. A lot of people look at me and see dumb Southern hick," he said with a shrug. "But I hope that I show others that I'm more than that."

I laughed at his description. "I think we're both a lot more than we seem. Even though, under normal circumstances, we'd be complete opposites."

"Then thank god for the campaign," Sam said, pulling me into him. "Otherwise, I would never have met you."

"Yes," I said, sinking into him. "Thank god for the campaign."

III

From that moment on, our summer was dedicated to the national convention. Unfortunately—or fortunately, depending on how you looked at it—the convention was in Milwaukee in the middle of July. Which meant that our entire office and as many volunteers as we could muster were supposed to drive into Milwaukee to be part of the process and fill seats.

I loved campaigns. From the outside, it might look frustrating. But from the inside, it was packaging a candidate into a believable platform and selling them to people like any other household product. It was taking something I believed in and making it consumable for others. People were twice as likely to vote every time they talked to someone about who they were going to vote for. They were even more likely to vote if someone knocked on their door or if they gave money to a candidate or if they volunteered for a campaign. Getting out there and organizing the campaign meant that I was having a literal impact on not just the campaign, but also the country. And it was worth it to me. The long hours and the high stress were all worth it.

But I hated the convention.

Yes, I wanted to see Woodhouse get nominated officially. The rest of the fanfare gave me a headache. A lot of pomp and posturing that did little to change anyone's mind. That money would be better off on the ground as far as I was concerned.

Not that I could say that to anyone but Sam and Moira as we got our volunteers off of the bus and directed them to their designated seats.

I was already tired by the time we snuck away with our staff badges to find a good place to grab a beer.

"I'm thinking beer and then a nap," I said with a yawn.

Moira nodded. "I'm down for that."

"Don't y'all want to see the nomination process?"

"No," Moira and I said in unison. Then we burst into laughter.

"Your loss," Sam said with a shrug.

"Oh, look, delegates," Moira said as we passed a group of men and women in expensive business suits, wearing floor credentials.

I scanned the crowd with excitement. These were

the people who actually got to cast the ballots for the primary nomination. It was purely a formality at this point, but still, it felt like an important job. And they got the best seats, too.

"I recognize a few of them," Sam said. "That guy is a state senator from North Carolina. That woman is a governor of, I think, Nevada. The redheaded man is the mayor of San Francisco."

Sam continued on, pointing out people that I'd had no idea how he knew. He must have had a knack for names and faces, or he studied this information extensively. It was damn impressive.

"Beer," Moira said, trying to pull him away. "You can fangirl later."

Sam laughed. "I'm not fangirling."

"Yes, you are," I said with a grin.

Then a voice called out from the crowd, "Lark!"

I glanced up, immediately on guard. Who the hell would know me here?

But then I saw a woman melt out of the crowd and stride toward me. She was a tall, imposing figure in a white power suit.

I heard Sam say next to me, "That's Leslie Kensington. She's a state senator in New York. She was barely defeated in her governor race a few years ago."

"I know," I said as I stepped up and embraced my best friend's mother. "Leslie, it's so good to see you."

"You too, dear. What are you doing here?" Leslie

asked. "I thought you were in New York."

I held up my staff credentials. "I'm working as a campaign organizer for Woodhouse in Madison."

"That's incredible," she said with a genuine smile. "I had no idea you had an interest in politics."

"I didn't either. I saw Woodhouse speak in the city last year and decided I had to join up. I'm loving the work though. It's very rewarding."

Leslie smiled at me. And my heart swelled. I hadn't realized that I'd missed my home so much. I hadn't had pangs of homesickness, but here, with Leslie, I felt different.

"I'm so glad you're doing it. We need hardworking people like you. What do your parents think?"

I waved away the question I had no intention of answering. "How's Penn? And Court?" I added hastily.

"You know my boys." Leslie rolled her eyes, avoiding the question as deftly as I'd avoided hers.

I laughed. "I sure do."

"Anyway, I have to return to my delegate duties. But when you come back to the city, come find me. I need some new, young talent. I'm thinking of running in the next mayoral race."

"Leslie," I gasped. "That's incredible. You'd be so great in that job."

Leslie patted my hand twice. "You're sweet. Seriously, come find me. If Woodhouse wants you, then so do I."

I grinned as she headed confidently back into the fray. When I turned back around, Moira and Sam were staring at me, slack-jawed. My smile faltered. I'd entirely forgotten they were standing there.

"Sorry about that. Beer?" I suggested.

"You know Leslie Kensington," Moira said, bouncing up and down. "And she offered you a job, working for her when she runs for the mayor of New York City. Lark, that's amazing!"

"Oh, thanks," I said with a half-smile.

"What an offer," Sam said, wrapping an arm around my shoulders as Moira directed the rest of the conversation and us to a bar.

When Moira went to get the first round, Sam and I settled into the last available table.

Silence stretched, and I finally got too anxious and broke it. "I'm not going to work for Leslie after this."

Sam furrowed his brows. "Why not? It sounds like a great opportunity."

"Well, maybe you could take it," I suggested.

He laughed. "I don't think it's transferable, Lark. And anyway, I'm going to apply to law schools."

I already had a JD. I'd gotten it so that I wouldn't have to start working for the company yet. My parents had indulged me. Just like they had with this. One day, I was going to have to stop running.

I looked down at my hands. "Well, actually, I made a deal with my parents."

"About what?"

"That I'd work here for a year on campaign, and then after that, I'd come home and takeover the company."

"Really? Is that what you want to do?"

"Yeah," I said unconvincingly, and then with more gusto, I continued, "Yes. Yes, of course. I've spent my entire life preparing for this. I wanted to grab ahold of more of my youth, you know? Once I start there, it's not like I can stop."

He put his hand on mine. "You know it's just me and you, right? You can tell me what you really feel."

I deflated. "I don't know, Sam. I thought for a long time that was what I wanted. And right now, that's the path I'm on. It's the family business. It's what I was born for. My parents aren't getting any younger. I don't want the board to have to take over when they decide to retire. It feels important."

He nodded. "Okay. If you say so."

"Maybe you could apply to NYU or Columbia Law," I suggested with excitement. "Then we could both be in the city."

"Yeah, maybe," he said softly.

Moira plunked three beers down in front of us at that moment. "Here we are! Drink up."

And we did. Letting the conversation slip away as easily as it had come.

FALL

I

The general election was a struck match.

One minute, nothing happened. The next, the entire world was on fire.

With only weeks to go before Election Day, we ran around as if we were all about to be burned. Like this was life or death. Our hours were extended. Our stress levels at max capacity. There was hardly enough time for me to see Sam outside of work. And when we did, we were zombies.

We'd all taken on assistants to ease the burden, but still, it wasn't enough. My first assistant had been a bit of a psychopath. She'd stolen someone's cat from their yard while canvassing and then lied about being sick to go out to eat with her friends for brunch. It obviously hadn't worked out. So, I was pretty desperate to get a new assistant.

I hadn't expected the one that I got—Melissa Young.

"Melissa," I said slowly. My eyes lifted to Sam's. "My assistant is Melissa Young. Why does that name sound familiar."

He cringed. "Uh...that's my ex-girlfriend."

"What?" I asked through gritted teeth.

"She messaged me and asked to join the campaign. She's out of school and wanted to help make a difference."

"So, you suggested she come here?" I asked with mild hysteria.

"No," he said at once. "I mean...yes, kind of."

"Sam!"

"Look, I can't turn down volunteers. I told her how to sign up. I had no idea that she was actually going to be assigned to work in our office."

I blew out a harsh breath. Great. Just great. This was going to be a disaster. But I could tell that Sam hadn't intended this to happen. Not that intentions meant anything when I was the one who was going to be saddled with his ex-girlfriend for the next two weeks.

Melissa showed up the next day.

"Oh my god," she cried. "You must be Lark."

She dragged me into a hug. She was a good five or six inches taller than me, and I didn't like how she hovered over me. I tried to fight back the urge to snap at her. I didn't know her. But as much as I wanted her gone, I also wanted to do the right thing and give her the benefit of the doubt. We had to survive each other for the next three weeks. I didn't want it to start off on the wrong foot.

"Hi," I said, withdrawing. "Yes, I'm Lark. And you're Melissa, I'm guessing."

"Yes! Of course. I'm Melissa. And I'm so glad to be here." She swiped her brown hair out of her heart-shaped face. She had the kind of smile that seemed to be plastered on.

"We're glad to have you," I lied. Then, I went for the truth. "I really need the help."

"That's what I heard!" she said, her Southern accent coming out on the edges of her words as she got animated. "Sam said this whole thing is exhausting, but I just had to be a part of it all. Too important not to be, right?"

I nodded once and bit my tongue. I'd been here for almost a year. I knew how important it was.

"So, you won't have your own office. But you can flit in and out of mine and use the open space as you will. We're a bit cramped," I told her.

"No worries. Where should I put my stuff?"

"Uh...over here." I gestured to my office that I still

shared with Sam despite Toby fighting to give us each our own space.

Luckily, Sam was out canvassing with a group of volunteers and wouldn't be back for a while.

Melissa deposited her suitcases into the office and dumped her giant purse on top of them. "All right," she said eagerly, her smile reaching her big brown eyes, "what do you need me to do? Put me to work!"

I assessed her and tried to be objective. Melissa seemed...nice. Even genuine. It surprised me. But I didn't know why.

Maybe because I had everything to lose. What I had with Sam, I'd never felt this way about anyone else, and the last thing I wanted was for Sam's ex to show up and take over. We had three more weeks to permanently be in each other's lives. I wanted to make it count. I didn't want to think about what would happen after.

I was pushing my own insecurities on Melissa. Maybe this wouldn't be so bad after all. Maybe I'd been stressed about all of this for no reason.

"All right, let's get started," I said with a smile.

"Well, what do you think?" Sam asked me later when we were seated at The Station with the rest of the office.

"Of Melissa?"

He nodded.

My gaze shifted to where she was animatedly talking to Moira as if they were long-lost friends. I sighed. "She seems really nice, Sam."

He laughed. "I knew you two would get along."

"I still think it's kind of weird," I admitted. "But she was a huge help today. She fit seamlessly into my established organization and took so much stress off of my shoulders."

"Good." He leaned forward and kissed me once on the lips. "I'm so glad, Lark. You really need the help."

"God, I really do," I agreed. "Especially after dealing with Virginia."

Sam groaned. "Virginia. What a nightmare."

"I still cannot believe that she tried to steal that person's cat."

He chuckled under his breath. "Like, what was she even thinking?"

"I have no idea. It's hilarious now, but when Maria called me in a panic because Virginia, my own paid assistant, had stolen someone's cat, it was awful. Calling Virginia and figuring out why the fuck she had stolen a cat and demanding she return it with an apology?" My head sank into my hands. "The worst."

Sam couldn't stop laughing. "It's probably the best-slash-worst thing that has happened on campaign."

"I'm glad that she's gone. She hated working but fooled everyone into thinking that she liked to work."

"Melissa will be better for you. She worked on campaigns back in North Carolina. She'll do a great job."

I looked at her one more time and nodded. "Yeah, I think you're right."

He patted my hand once and then stood. "I'm going to the restroom. If they come back with my fries, try not to eat them all before I get back."

I grinned devilishly. "No promises."

He shook his head at me as he walked away.

As soon as he was gone, Melissa plopped down in front of me. "Hey there, boss."

"Hey. How was your first day?"

"Great, great," she said cheerfully. Then, she conspiratorially leaned forward. "So, between us girls, are you and Sam serious?"

"Uh, yeah," I said, warning signs blaring. This was not a good conversation. I needed to back away slowly.

"And you think...what? You'll stay together after the campaign?"

There was something else in Melissa's brown eyes now. Deceit.

"That's the plan," I ground out.

Melissa laughed softly. "That's cute."

"What is?" I asked despite myself.

"Sam doesn't do long distance." She shrugged her

shoulders as if she were sympathetic. "So, if you go back to New York, that's that." She wiped her hands together twice.

"I think I'm done with this conversation," I said, rising to my feet.

Melissa smiled dangerously as she stood to meet me. "We might work together, Lark, but I'm here for Sam. He's going to be mine. By the end of this, I'm going to win him back."

Something snapped inside of me. The Upper East Side bitch inside who didn't take shit, who could eat someone like Melissa Young for breakfast. I channeled that girl who owned Manhattan and knew that Melissa stood no chance against Larkin St. Vincent.

I leaned in real close and gave her my best eat-shit-and-die look. "If you try, Melissa," I crooned, "I'll ruin your life."

Then I pushed back from the table and went to sit with Moira instead. My blood was boiling. I wanted to tell Sam, to get it all out in the open, but Melissa would deny it. I was sure of it. And it would make me look bad.

No, we'd handle this between us girls.

If she made a move on my boyfriend, she'd find out that hers wouldn't be the first life I'd ruined. And I followed through on *all* of my promises.

II

Fall in Wisconsin was way too cold for my sensibilities. I was used to perfect New York falls, and this did not cut it.

I shivered as I stepped out of my Subaru and entered the office. It was swamped. With so little time until Election Day, our schedules were jam-packed. I wished that I were doing something mindless right then. Instead, I'd sent Melissa out to canvass and not heard from her in hours. She hadn't responded to any of my texts or calls.

I stuck my head into my joint office with Sam. "Hey," I said when I saw him inside.

"Lark, you're back," he said with a smile. "I thought you'd be on campus all day."

"Well, I would be, but I can't find Melissa. She was supposed to be canvassing. I had her down as a team lead this afternoon. But I haven't seen her in hours. Have you seen her?"

"Shit, she didn't call?"

My brows furrowed. "About what?"

Sam ran a hand back through his hair. "Her volunteer housing fell through."

"What?" I asked, confused and also suspicious. "Already? It's only been a few days."

"I know. She came here freaking out because the volunteer had to get her out within the hour. I guess the guy was a real jerk about it."

"That doesn't even make sense. All of the housing is vetted months in advance. How would that happen?"

"I don't know, Lark. But it did. It was awful. She was a crying mess when she talked to me. I helped her get out of there as fast as she could."

My stomach knotted at those words. "Did you talk to Toby? What house is she staying at now?"

He shook his head. "I didn't even think. I kind of... invited her to stay with me."

I straightened. "You did what?"

"She was in such a horrible place. I figured, it's two weeks, and she can crash on my couch like I did at yours."

"We hooked up the entire time you stayed on my couch," I reminded him.

His cheeks turned red. "That's not what I meant, and you know it."

"What I know is that you're letting your ex-girl-friend stay in your apartment, Sam."

He sighed. "Fuck. Lark, I swear it's not a big deal."

He couldn't be that naive to think that Melissa wasn't playing the long game. He really believed her bullshit that something had happened with her housing. It sucked because he didn't see it.

"Sam," I groaned. "What are you doing?"

He stood and pulled me to him. "I'm not doing anything. I'm just being nice. You know I love you."

"I do," I whispered.

"Melissa is staying for two weeks on my couch. We're never home, except to pass out. I swear it isn't going to be a big deal. Why don't you come over tonight and see for yourself?"

I really, really didn't want to do that. But I also *had* to do that. Because I knew that Melissa was after Sam, and this was the start of her game plan. I needed to be there to cockblock her. To show her that he was already mine.

I nodded. "Fine. Okay. But I still don't like it."

"I understand, but I'll show you that it's nothing. Promise."

He kissed me, and I almost believed him.

"Wait, you're telling me that your boyfriend is letting his ex-girlfriend stay in his apartment?" one of my best friends, Katherine asked over the phone.

I paced my bedroom in frustration.

As soon as I'd gotten home, I'd called Katherine. It was late, but she was a socialite and never slept. I had known she'd be up and available to talk. And also, she was maybe the most dangerous, conniving person I knew.

"Yes," I muttered. "It's a disaster."

"Tell the bitch to move the fuck out, Lark."

"As much as I'd love to do that, I think it'd hurt Sam. He's never seen me act that way."

Katherine laughed. "He sounds like a nice guy."

"He is."

"Nice guys bulldozer hearts," Katherine told me. "And they do it with a smile on their face."

"I don't think they're hooking up or anything. But I don't want Melissa to make a move on him."

"You know what I'd do?"

I sighed. I knew where this was going. "What's that, Katherine?"

"Establish dominance. If you don't, she will."

I tipped my head up to the ceiling. "I don't think playing a game of What Would Katherine Do is productive."

"That means, you'd win. Now, buck up, St.

Vincent," Katherine said with a tinkling laugh. "Go get your man."

I laughed and then ended the call. Katherine was a bit of a head case, but she was basically family, and I loved her. Her pep talks worked, too. I was already feeling better.

And I did know what I needed to do.

I hastily changed out of work clothes and into a sexy off-the-shoulder sweater and skintight jeans. Then, I drove over to Sam's place. I knocked once and then let myself inside. Melissa's suitcases were pushed into a corner. She was seated on the couch in what I guessed were her pajamas—a teeny-tiny tank top and even smaller shorts. She had to be freezing, considering the lows right now were in the thirties.

"Hey, Lark," Melissa said with her sugary-sweet smile.

Sam came out of the back bedroom in gray sweats and a hoodie. "Hey, you made it."

"Yeah, I had to get out of work clothes."

Sam covered his mouth as he yawned. "I get that. You look good."

"Thanks," I said, walking toward him.

He put his hands on my hips as I stood on my toes to press a kiss to his mouth. I definitely shouldn't have listened to Katherine's advice. But I could practically feel Melissa squirming behind me. So, it felt worth it.

I gently pushed him back into the bedroom. He

laughed softly as I toed the door closed behind us. The connotation was clear. *Mine, mine, mine.*

My hands slid under his hoodie, and I grazed his toned abs with my nails.

"What are you doing?" he asked with that perfect Sam smile.

"Touching you."

"Right now? I thought you were here to see that everything was fine. We've been home for, like, twenty minutes, and I'm ready to crash."

"Uh-huh," I said, running a finger along the waist-band of his sweats.

He shuddered under my touch. "I think you have something else on your mind."

I bit my lip. "That obvious, huh?"

I stood on my toes again and firmly pressed my lips against his. He pulled me close at the heat in the kiss, and I could tell that I had him.

"Okay," he whispered against me. "As long as we're quiet."

"Oh, I can be quiet," I murmured as quiet as a mouse.

"You generally are not."

I sank my hand into his pants and ran down the length of him. "Neither are you."

He gasped at the first touch. "Fair."

"I know what I want," I told him as I angled his body toward the wall and pushed him up against it.

K.A. LINDE

His eyes were wide with surprise and hunger. He was not stopping me, even as his back thumped against the wall. Loud enough for anyone on the other side to hear.

"What's that?" he got out. His Adam's apple bobbed.

Slowly, I sank to my knees before him. His eyes went wide as I dragged his sweats and boxers down his legs, letting his cock jut out in front of my face.

"Lark," he groaned as I stroked him and licked my lips.

I leaned forward and took the tip of him in my mouth. His cock jumped in my mouth as I bobbed forward against him. My tongue laved the shaft before coming back and concentrating on the head.

"Fuck," he said. "Fuck, fuck, fuck."

Not a single word was quiet.

I braced myself against his hips as I sucked him off. And despite whatever reason this had all started, I was getting turned on just from doing this. His body was responding so perfectly. Getting bigger and thicker inside my mouth. His hands were buried in my hair. Not quite guiding me, but not exactly leaving me fully to my own capacities either.

I could tell as he tightened his grip on my head that he was getting close. His cock jerked in my mouth. He thrust forward slightly once, twice as he came so close to climax.

86

My jaw ached, and I nearly gagged as he got deeper and deeper into my mouth. But I wasn't going to stop.

"Close," was the only word he got out before he came into my mouth.

I squeezed my eyes shut before swallowing it down.

"Fuck, Lark," he said. He was practically shaking from his orgasm. His eyes were heavy-lidded and sex-driven.

"I like when you say my name like that."

He bent down and lifted me to my feet. Then he stepped out of his clothes and pushed me back to the bed. It squeaked noisily with every movement. I smiled as it squealed beneath me.

"Your turn."

I bit my lip. "I'm not sure I can be quiet for that."

He was already moving to my jeans and grinned. "As quiet as you can," he said before burying his face between my legs.

I was not quiet. At all.

III

I stayed over at Sam's every night that week. I trusted him. But I didn't trust Melissa one bit. Not even a little. Not after she'd told me that she was going after him. I didn't want to give her the opportunity for an in.

My phone started buzzing as I groggily made it to campus. I checked the number and saw that it was Katherine. I yawned and sent it to voicemail. I had a meeting with my volunteer Kennedy about final poll schedules. She'd been having some trouble with a group of core volunteers who had started to get flaky. End-of-the-semester blues or something. And I wanted to get it worked out ASAP.

My meeting with Kennedy lasted about a half hour. I pulled my phone back out to call Katherine and stared down at it in shock.

"What?" Kennedy asked in surprise.

"I have, like, a dozen missed calls," I told her.

"Did someone die?"

I shook my head. "I have no idea."

My parents had called. Twice. *All* of my friends had called—Katherine, Penn, Lewis, and Rowe. Even people I wasn't as friendly with were listed in my missed calls.

"What the fuck?" I whispered. "I'm going to call my friend back."

"No problem. Let me know if something's wrong or you need my help," she said, packing up her bag and heading out.

Just as I went to call Katherine, my closest friend from law school, Anna English, called. We spoke every week, but this wasn't when she normally called.

"English," I said uncertainly. "What's up?"

"Lark, how are you?"

"I don't know. What happened?"

English was silent a second. "You haven't seen?"

"Seen?"

"All right, I hate to be the one to break it to you. But I check TMZ on the regular now for my new job."

"Oh, right...you're a publicist now. But...TMZ?"

"Yeah." English cleared her throat. "So, you're in a rather, um...unflattering picture, which just showed up in the tabloids. The headline reads, *Upper East Side Princess in the Dirt.*"

My hands shook. "What?"

"Yeah, I guess someone found out that you were campaigning. And instead of talking about it like it was a good thing, they posted a shit picture of you an article about how you're slumming it. It's really disgusting."

"Oh my god," I whispered in horror. "Does it say who gave them the information or the picture?"

"No, I've been digging, but it looks like it was an anonymous tip."

"Fuck," I muttered.

"I'm so sorry. I'm going to see if the PR firm can do anything about it, but...it's already circulating."

"And the internet is forever."

"Pretty much."

I swallowed back bile. "Thanks, English. Thanks for letting me know."

"Of course. I'm so sorry. If there's anything else I can do, let me know."

"I will. You're the best."

We said our good-byes. This could not be happening. I'd done everything right. I hadn't wanted anyone to know what I was doing. When you were the heir to a Fortune 500 company, you took precautions to hide your identity. I didn't care if Sam knew, but I hadn't wanted the *world* to know.

I clicked over to my texts and found a link to the

article in one of them. My stomach dropped as I read the rest of the text. It was short, no more than two paragraphs, but it was disgusting. I'd been in the media a fair amount, especially in high school when I ran wild. But this was a new level of low. I was here, doing a good thing, and they made it look like I was doing something wrong. Ugh!

Then my eyes scanned the picture, which really could not have been less flattering. I tilted my head and narrowed my eyes. Wait. I remembered what I'd been doing when I wore that outfit a few days ago. To have gotten that shot, it had to have been someone who was volunteering for the campaign.

My body froze as my sickness turned to anger. Melissa. It had to be Melissa. This was how she was fighting. I had no idea how she knew who I really was, but there was no other explanation. I'd been working with most of these volunteers for months. There'd be no reason for them to turn me in...if they even knew who I was. But Melissa had motive.

I shook my head. I couldn't believe this.

I sent the article to Sam and then dialed his number. I knew that he was busy, but this couldn't wait.

"Hey, Lark. Can I call you back in five?" he asked as soon as he answered.

"Melissa sold a picture of me to the tabloids."

"What?" he asked in shock. He cleared his throat

and then said something to his volunteers. "I'm free. Now, tell me what's going on."

"I sent you the article in a text. She sold me out to the tabloids."

Sam was silent for a minute. "I just read the article, and it's fucking trash, Lark. Everything posted there is utter bullshit."

"I know," I whispered. Not that it made me feel any better.

"But why do you think Melissa did this? It could have been anyone."

"I've been on campaign for almost a year, Sam. The only thing that's changed is her. And she was *there* that day when I was wearing that outfit."

Sam sighed. "Lark, I love you, but breathe for a minute. You don't really know Melissa. She is a sweet, kind Southern girl. This is not her style *at all*."

"Then I think that you don't really know her, Sam. Because this has her name all over it."

"Look," he said with another sigh, "we are a week away from Election Day. You haven't slept in months, and you're not feeling that great."

Which was true. I'd woken up yesterday with some horrible cold that wouldn't leave.

"Maybe let your volunteers take over and try to relax."

"Sam," I groaned.

"Please, Lark. The election will be over soon, and

after a few days of sleep, we'll all be able to see more clearly. Okay?"

"Okay," I lied.

"I have to get back, but call me if you need me. I love you."

"I love you, too."

I hung up the phone and dropped my head back. He wouldn't even listen to me. He thought it was the cold and sleep deprivation talking. But I hadn't told him that Melissa claimed to be here to win him back. Not that he'd likely believe *that* either.

But I *knew* she had done this. I fucking knew it.

If she wanted to play dirty, I could show her what the Upper East Side was really like. Show Sam exactly what Melissa was capable of.

IV

"Hey, Lark," Melissa said with a cheeky smile as she showed up on campus later that day.

I could see in her keen eyes that she was anticipating my reaction.

"Melissa," I said with a head nod. "I'm waiting for a few more volunteers, and then I'll have you take them out to canvass."

"Oh, yeah? You don't want me for training today?" She dropped her backpack down with a clunk.

"No, I think you'll be needed in the field."

Melissa opened her mouth like she was going to argue, but I turned away from her and handed out a clipboard to one of the volunteers. She wasn't going to get a reaction from me. I wasn't going to let her think that she'd gotten to me. But I also wasn't going to reward her behavior by letting her stay here and train volunteers, which half the time meant she sat around on her laptop. I had other people I trusted to do trainings. I wanted her out of my sight.

When everyone was finally here, I paired people off and then sent them out into the field. Melissa hovered by me.

"Do you need something?"

"I saw that horrible article about you this morning."

I blinked. "Okay?"

"You must be feeling awful."

I laughed softly, glad that Melissa hadn't been on campus earlier when I had my breakdown. "I'm from the Upper East Side. Much worse has been said about me. Those tabloids are trash anyway."

"Right. Do you know who did that?" she asked, wide-eyed with innocence.

I just smiled. "We both know who did it."

Melissa arched her eyebrows. "I don't know what you're insinuating."

"Why don't you go work?" I suggested. "You're not really needed here."

Melissa pursed her lips. Then she leaned in close. "You didn't think I'd let you get away with saying you were going to ruin my life, did you?"

I said nothing. Just kept my steady gaze on her. It didn't matter that she'd confirmed that she'd done it.

I'd already known that. And Sam wouldn't believe me either way. Not now. Not yet.

"Have a nice day," I said, turning my back on her.

She hovered behind me a second before huffing off after another volunteer. Good riddance.

I dropped into my chair, thankful that everyone had disappeared for the next couple hours. I downed some more cold medicine and blew my nose, and then I went to work. But no matter how much I tried to focus, my mind kept spinning back to Melissa. I needed something to get back at her. To prove that she wasn't what she seemed.

My gaze wandered to her backpack. I bit my lip and then drew it toward me. I fished out her laptop and then opened it in front of me.

Password.

Crap.

I had no clue what it could be. Luckily, one of my crew was a tech genius. Rowe had invented the social media platform Crew, which was sweeping the country right now. I'd seen him hack people in minutes in high school. He'd know how to do it.

I dialed his number.

"Lark," he said in greeting. "I've been trying to get rid of that picture all morning."

Leave it to Rowe to cut straight to the issue. "Thanks, Rowe. But I need to get into someone's computer, but it's password-protected. How do I get around that?"

"Is it a company computer?"

"No. Just a personal laptop."

"Mac?"

"Yeah."

"Okay. Here is what you do," he began.

He didn't care one bit *why* I needed to break into a computer. He'd always had ambiguous morals about tech security. Classic Rowe.

I carefully followed his instructions and was shocked that within a few keystrokes, I'd bypassed the password, and I was into Melissa's laptop. Damn, that had been almost too easy.

"Thanks, Rowe."

"Anytime. I'll keep working on the picture."

I laughed. "Thanks."

I didn't know what I was looking for as I dug through her computer files. Something, anything incriminating. I found a ton of pictures, including dozens with some guy named Joey. They were recent, too. None of them were dirty, but it was a start. I pulled up the browser and opened her Crew account, which she stayed logged in to. I searched for Joey in her Friends list and found the same guy. He lived in Chapel Hill, but his profile was basically empty. No pictures of him with Melissa. No relationship status. I frowned and decided to try her email.

When I typed *Joey* into the search bar, dozens of emails popped up. Bingo.

From some digging through her emails, I gathered that they'd met on Tinder and been hooking up for weeks. It looked like neither of them had put a label on it, and she'd put him on hold while she was out of town. On hold but not finished.

I quickly forwarded their conversations to my email so I could read them later and then deleted it from her sent file. I checked the time with excitement coursing through me. Most people got sick at the thought of doing something dangerous, but a part of me relished it. A part of me wanted to destroy things. I'd spent the last year with Sam, pushing down the darker sides of my personality. Just trying to be Lark. But Larkin St. Vincent got shit *done*.

Then I drafted an email to Joey, copying Melissa's writing style.

Hey,

How are you? Hope you're doing well. I know that the campaign ends in a week, but I've really been missing you. I wish that you could come up to Wisconsin and visit. A girl can dream, right?

Mel

My heart pattered in my chest as I hit the Send button and waited for a response. From previous email exchanges, it looked like he was always on his email, waiting for her to send something. I'd thought it was weird that they weren't texting, but apparently, at his job, he couldn't use his phone. Hence the hundreds of emails.

The screen blinked, and a new message appeared.

Mel,

It's good to hear from you. It's so boring here without you. I've really missed you, too. Are you serious about me coming to visit?

Joey

I responded next, sticking to how they normally talked back and forth.

Dead serious. Do you think you could make it work? —Mel

Gah, I can get the time off work, but I checked the flights, and they're crazy. I don't think that I could afford to do it. —Joey

I tapped my lip. I had a solution to that, but it

was mad.

I could pay for your flight. I have more money coming in right now. I wouldn't mind. —Mel

Nah. I could never accept that. Though it would be so worth it. —Joey

I smiled devilishly. *Here we go.*

But I want to. Just send me your info, and I'll book it for Saturday morning. —Mel

You're sure? —Joey

You said it yourself. It'd be so worth it. —Mel

I tapped my finger on the keyboard, waiting. Melissa wouldn't be back for at least another hour, but still, the nerves were making me jittery.

All right. I'll come. —Joey

My smile grew at the response.
Hook, line, and sinker.
I knew how I was going to take down Melissa Young. She would regret ever releasing that picture of me or thinking she could take Sam from me.

V

I couldn't shake my cold. My head felt like it was a thousand pounds, my throat was scratchy, and my entire face was stuffy. And that was *with* medicine.

"You should really go to the doctor," Sam said as I blew my nose for the hundredth time.

"I'll be fine," I said, my voice nasally.

"You are not fine. You're not sleeping. Your body is shutting down."

I pressed my hand to my head. "When am I going to have time to go to the doctor, Sam? It's three days until the election. I have to be here."

"Even this isn't worth killing yourself over," he reminded me.

I sank into a seat at the front of the office. I didn't even have it in me to argue. My eyes were hot and heavy. Though I was pretty sure that I didn't have a fever. Just this stupid cold.

"Ready to go to campus?" Melissa asked, trotting into the office with a bounce in her step.

"Lark isn't going to campus today," Sam said. "She's too sick."

"Oh nooo," Melissa crooned. "That is too bad, Lark."

I glared up at her. "I'm going to campus."

"You're going to a doctor."

"No," I told him flatly.

"Lark," he groaned.

The door to the office opened again, and a bell jingled overhead, cutting Sam off. In walked a tall, burly guy with glasses. My mouth went dry.

Joey.

"Melissa!" he said cheerfully. Then he strode across the room and scooped her up in a hug.

I saw panic skitter across her face before disappearing. She pushed him away as soon as he put her down.

"Who the hell are you?" she gasped.

Joey looked at her in confusion. "Mel, it's me, Joey."

Melissa just blinked. "You must be mistaken. I have no idea who you are. I've never seen you a day in my life."

If I'd been feeling better, I would have gaped. Melissa was a damn good actress. How was she faking this so well?

Sam glanced between them and then put his hand out, ever the Southern gentleman. "Hey, man, I'm Sam."

Joey shook his hand. "Uh...Joey."

"I'm not sure what's going on here," Sam said. "Are you a volunteer for the campaign?"

Joey looked between them, confusion written across his features. "Well, see, Melissa here is my girlfriend. She invited me to come see her at the end of the campaign."

"I did no such thing," Melissa said automatically.

Joey furrowed his brows. "Don't know why you're pretending not to know me, Mel. You're the one who bought the ticket."

Melissa's eyes rounded. "Uh, no, I didn't."

"Hey, man, maybe there was some kind of misunderstanding," Sam said, trying to play peacekeeper.

"No misunderstanding," Joey drawled. "I have the emails here." He found the emails we'd sent back and forth and handed them to Melissa.

She scanned the emails, and Sam glanced over her shoulder.

"That's your email," Sam reasoned.

"I must have been hacked!" Melissa cried. "I wouldn't do this. Does this even sound like me, Sam?"

He shrugged like he didn't want to get involved even though he was already involved. "Y'all can figure that out."

K.A. LINDE

Melissa whipped around on Joey. "You said I paid for the flight? Do you have the receipt?"

My stomach twisted. Oh god. I'd deleted everything else. I'd even blocked Joey after our final interaction so that Melissa wouldn't get more emails from him. But the receipt...shit, could that be incriminating? I'd run everything by Rowe. We'd both thought that I'd covered my tracks.

Joey handed her his phone again.

"Ha!" she cried. "The last four digits of my credit card are 3711, not 5512." She pulled out her wallet and showed everyone. "I didn't do this."

Sam looked even more confused. "So...what happened?"

"Obviously, someone hacked my email." Melissa took a step away from Joey. "They invented this boyfriend, which I never had, and paid for him to come and humiliate me."

"That sounds...outrageous, Mel. Who would ever do that?"

Melissa froze, and then her eyes found mine. I had been carefully blank through the entire interaction. Just holding a tissue to my nose and trying not to fall over from exhaustion.

"Oh my god, *you* did this," Melissa accused me.

"Mel, come on," he said.

I cringed at the way he'd used her nickname. I didn't like the sound of it in his mouth.

Then the little actress burst into tears. She began to cry into her hands. I had to fight back rolling my eyes.

"It's Lark. Sam, she's...she's out to *get* me," she cried dramatically. "She told me the first day that I met her that if I got near you, she'd ruin my life. Now, look what she did!"

Sam put his arm around her and patted her shoulder. I glared at the exchange.

"I did no such thing," I managed to get out.

My head was pounding even harder. Everything felt fuzzy.

Melissa ripped herself out of Sam's embrace and lunged for my purse. If I'd been feeling better, I might have been able to stop her. But as it was, I was too slow. I couldn't get it quick enough. Then she snatched out my wallet. Sam was telling her to stop, but she didn't listen. She reached in and wrenched out my credit cards until she gasped.

"Look." She threw the card at Sam.

His eyes widened as he looked down at the credit card in his hand.

"5512," Melissa spat. Then she started crying again. "I *told* you she was out to get me! I told you! All of this is a farce. She made it all up."

"Sam, I..." I got out as I tried to stand. But I quickly sank back down. Standing was too much effort. Fuck.

Sam's look of disbelief broke my heart. "Lark, did you...did you do this?"

"Sam..."

"Did you?"

"Of course she did," Melissa said, sobbing.

Joey looked uncomfortable, like he wanted to back out of the room.

"Melissa...Melissa started it," I forced out. My stomach twisted. Fear spiked through my veins.

Oh god, that look in his eyes. That look that said he had no idea who I was. It was too much. I needed to get up. I needed to say more.

He glanced between us. "I don't know what is going on here, but I don't want any part of it."

"Melissa wrote that article in the tabloids. She sent them the picture. She told me herself!" I told him. "She told me when she first showed up that she was here to win you back. This all started because of what she did."

Sam shook his head. He looked disgusted. "I really don't know what's true. But this is your credit card. This proof is in front of my face."

"Sam..." I pleaded.

"We have an election to win," he said gruffly. He stuffed the card back in my wallet and tossed it on top of my purse. "We all need to get to work."

With one more glance at me and then Melissa, he strode out of the office. If I'd felt an ounce better, I would have rushed after him. I'd have explained what happened and why I'd done what I'd done. But I could barely scramble to my feet. By the time I got to the door, his truck was already peeling out of the parking lot.

Melissa came to step up next to me. A cruel smile painted her lips. She didn't say a word. Just threw her shoulder into mine, making me stumble and nearly fall with the weight of my sickness. Then she strode out after him.

Leaving me all alone with Joey and how everything had just completely blown up in my face. The realization of what I'd done...what I'd lost.

I felt cold.

Like I was drowning in a frozen lake.

I'd ruined everything.

Everything.

VI

A beer sat untouched in front of me. I'd arrived at The Station a half hour ago when Toby told me there was nothing more that could be done. Election results were on every screen in the bar. Wisconsin hadn't been called yet, but most of the East Coast had. Woodhouse was ahead by *a lot.* We were just waiting for the final outcome.

Moira slid into the seat across from me. "You look like you're feeling better."

I glanced up at her and shrugged. My cold was mostly gone, which I found shocking, considering my mental health had completely deteriorated after Sam walked out of the office. I hadn't seen him since.

"So, what happened with you and Sam?" Moira asked gently. "People said there was a screaming match and lots of crying."

I shook my head. "I don't know, Moira. I blew it."

"I can't imagine whatever happened being serious enough to wreck you two. You've been inseparable for the last *year*."

"I know." I sighed. "I don't know what to do."

She tipped her head behind me. "Fix it."

I turned around to find Sam walking into The Station. He looked around the room until he found me and then beelined in my direction. Just as he reached me, the entire room went up in chaos. We both turned to the TVs. Wisconsin had been called for Woodhouse. *And with Wisconsin, so goes the country.*

"We won," Sam said to me.

"So it appears," I said.

Everyone else around us was hugging and cheering and congratulating. Toasts were made. Drinks were chugged. Celebration ensued. And Sam and I stared at each other in silence. This was not celebratory. I could see it on his face. This was not fixable in his eyes. I knew it before he said a word.

"Was it real?" he asked.

I swallowed and nodded. "Of course. Yes."

"Which Lark is the real one?" he continued. "Were you acting with me the last year?"

"No, Sam. I'm sorry about what happened. But what we had was real."

He sighed and glanced away. "You didn't trust me."

"I didn't trust Melissa."

"Semantics," he said. "You went behind my back to hurt Melissa because you thought that we were going to get back together. You didn't trust me."

"I don't know what to say, Sam. You invited her to *live* with you. You knew I was uncomfortable. And you didn't hear me when I tried to warn you."

"So, you decided to try to ruin her life?" he demanded. "Lark, that's..." He shook his head again and crossed his arms. Closed off. "I'm going back to North Carolina."

My stomach dropped. We'd never said what would happen next after the campaign. I'd said that I had to hold to my promise to my parents and he was applying to law schools. He could have stayed with me in New York while he applied. He could have chosen NYU or Columbia or even Fordham. Anywhere nearby. But now...he was going home.

"When?"

"In two days. Melissa is driving back with me in the truck."

I thought I was going to be sick. "So, with Melissa then?"

Just as I'd always suspected.

"She lives there, too."

"Sam, please," I gasped.

He looked away as if he couldn't witness my pain.

"What about us?"

His gaze fell to his feet. "I don't think there is an us. Not when neither of us can trust the other."

I choked back a sob. "What am I going to do without you?"

"You're going to go back to New York," he told me with a sad smile. "You're going to join your parents and run your empire. Wasn't that always the plan anyway?"

I nodded but felt utterly hollow inside. It *was* the plan. But I couldn't imagine going home without him. Sam would never come to my city. It'd be empty, just like my life.

He looked like he wanted to reach out and hug me one last time. I stepped forward, hoping for it, hoping to find the words to change his mind. Except he didn't want to change his mind. The last year had been an adventure, but the adventure was over. I would go back to being Larkin St. Vincent, heiress to a fortune, an Upper East Side princess. And he'd return to Chapel Hill. He'd go to law school and build houses with his dad. He'd get back together with Melissa.

Our lives diverged like a river. Maybe we had never been meant to cross in the first place.

"Good-bye, Lark," he said, not able to hide the hitch in his voice before he turned and walked back out of The Station.

Movers came the next day to pack up my apartment. I just had to fill a suitcase, say good-bye to the rest of my colleagues, and then get on a plane back to New York. I lingered anyway, hoping to see Sam one last time. Moira pulled me into a hug and promised to stay close. I agreed. Though I wanted to leave everything about this campaign behind me. Without Sam, how could I even think about it?

So, I left the office and headed to the Madison airport. I boarded in first class and tried to sleep as I flew back home alone. Everything ached, and even a drink didn't silence the demons.

This wasn't what I'd wanted. This wasn't supposed to happen.

Sam was my first love.

My first everything.

We were supposed to drive off into the sunset together. Not end up torn down the middle. I wasn't supposed to feel sick to my stomach every time I thought about him.

And worse, this was my fault. Not completely. Not all of it. He'd still invited Melissa. He'd still let her stay at his place. He'd still believed Melissa over me...every time. But I'd done horrible, horrible things to try to keep him. When I should have realized he was mine and he had no intention of letting me go. Until I'd shown him who I truly was.

My whole life, I'd gotten by with my name and my

money. This was the first time ever that someone had loved me for who I was, with no pretense. And then my old self had reared its ugly head and destroyed the best thing in my life.

Bad Lark.

That was what had happened. I'd become Bad Lark.

She felt like a separate entity to who I really was. And I wanted to be rid of her. I didn't want to fall into that trap. I never, *ever* wanted to be Bad Lark again.

I felt stronger when I got off the plane than when I'd boarded. Still hollow and empty where Sam's light had previously shone through me. But free of the person I'd been, the one who had sent those emails to Joey and destroyed her own life.

Instead, I was just *me*.

And that was who I was going to be for everyone from now on.

When I wheeled my suitcase out to baggage claim, I broke into a smile. There, standing inside LaGuardia Airport, was my crew. Katherine in a skimpy red dress. Penn dressed in a suit, his eyes lost and contemplative. Rowe fiddling with his iPad. Lewis perfectly put together, as normal. He noticed me first and burst into a giant smile as he waved.

I walked toward them, and they all drew me into a hug at once. Even Rowe, who hated touching. I laughed.

"You're all here," I said in surprise.

"Of course," Penn said with command. "You were gone for a year. We missed you."

"We did," Lewis agreed.

"Yeah, I'm tired of being *completely* outnumbered," Katherine said with an eye roll.

I looked around at my friends—my family. At least I wasn't alone. They'd always loved me for exactly who I was. They'd seen me at my best and my worst. And they wouldn't care which Lark appeared before them that day.

But as I walked out of the airport with my friends, my heart still panged for Sam. And I knew it would be a long, *long* time until I got over him.

If I *ever* did.

Continue Lark & Sam's story in *USA Today* bestselling author K.A. Linde's second chance romance...

CRUEL TRUTH

Available now!
Turn the page to read a sneak peek!

CRUEL TRUTH
CHAPTER 1 — LARK

"Larkin, darling, I don't understand why you're mad," my mother said. She turned crisply in her sharp Chanel suit that hugged her figure perfectly.

"You don't understand anything apparently," I snapped back.

I nudged a pile of boxes as high as my head that had manifested in my living room out of thin air. It was six thirty in the morning. I hadn't had my coffee. And I was ready to combust.

"I am just trying to keep you up-to-date on the latest fashions. If you're a part of this family, then you must look the part of a St. Vincent, dear."

"Get them out of here, Mother. I don't need seventeen pairs of high heels," I growled, estimating the boxes in front of me, "or thirty evening gowns or twenty new handbags. Mother, I work on the mayor's campaign. This isn't my *life* anymore."

"Nonsense," she said. "Who doesn't want more clothes? I did find you a dozen new power suits to replace that number you're wearing right now." She pointed up and down at me. "It'll do you wonders."

I ground my teeth and debated whether or not this was worth the fight. My mother, Hope St. Vincent, cared about next to nothing in this world other than appearances. She still probably wondered how she had gotten so unlucky to have a daughter who didn't want to take over the family business and live the same life she presently lived on the Upper East Side—filthy rich, married, and miserable. I swore, my parents hadn't shared a bed in twenty years. The St. Vincents took *fucked up* to a whole new level.

"I honestly cannot handle you right now," I said. "Please have this all cleared out. I have to get to work."

"All this work causes you so much stress." My mother strutted over to me on her six-inch Louboutins and pressed her fingers to my forehead. "There's this new plastic surgeon everyone is talking about. I could get you a Botox appointment. It's preventative!"

I counted slowly to ten, reminding myself this was my mother and that somewhere deep, *deep* down she meant well.

"I'm leaving." I reached for my bag. "Also, I'm

having the locks changed. I don't even know how you got *in* here."

"Oh, Larkin, you're overreacting, as always."

Any minute now, she would be inviting me to early morning martinis. It was never too early to drink.

"As you know, Mayor Kensington's reelection campaign is gearing up," I reminded her as patiently as I could. "I have even less time than normal to do anything. Today, I have a huge meeting about the mayoral fundraising banquet next week. So, I have to go."

"Oh, of course," my mother said. "Leslie told me about that. We purchased a table, obviously." She opened a box and pulled out a lavender St. Vincent's handbag. My mother's signature bag—the Larkin. I cringed. God, it had been a nightmare, growing up with my name on a bag. She shoved the bag into my hand. "Too bad that Nina isn't going anymore."

"It is too bad," I agreed.

Then I tossed the Larkin bag back into the box. I was not looking forward to my parents being at the banquet. It made my job so much harder.

My mother continued to fish through the new clothes and pick things out. Sometimes, I dreamed that I was adopted. It was just a fantasy though. My mother and I had the same signature chestnut-red hair. Though she kept it long and straight as a board while mine curled every which way if I let it. And under her layers of makeup, she had the same heart-shaped face, the same pouty lips, and the same bright green eyes as me. I had once thought that we had the same smile, but my mother didn't really smile anymore.

It pained me to think that I'd once been so vapid. The Upper East Side took everyone as its victim. I'd been trying so hard to stay out of that life. Except for my closest friends—my crew, the four people in my life who were more like family than my own parents—I stayed out of the madness. But somehow, it always sucked me back in. Just like my mother tried to do right this very minute.

"Okay. You figure out what to do with all these clothes," I said on a sigh. I knew it was stupid to give in to her. For every inch, she took a mile. But I had to leave. I had too much work to do to deal with this right now. "I'm going to go to work."

"Oh, take the limo!"

I shook my head. "I'll grab a cab."

"Don't be absurd. Your father's Mercedes is only two blocks over. He can pick me up, and you'll be free with the limo."

"That's okay. I'll take a cab. It'll be fine," I said, grabbing my own purse and striding toward the door.

"Will we see you for brunch?"

I rolled my eyes. "Depends on how busy I am after the banquet this weekend! I'll talk to you later."

With a sigh, I pushed out of my door and hurried

to the elevator. Dear god, I thought somewhere in my brain that it would get easier to deal with my parents. That someday, they would come to accept that I actually enjoyed working on campaigns. That I liked being a campaign manager for the mayor of New York City. It didn't help that my parents ran St. Vincent's Resorts, a multibillion-dollar company that had been in my family for generations. Or that my mother had created St. Vincent handbags and cosmetics. Not only did they want me to take over the family business, they also had a long list of suitors they found acceptable for me to marry. They didn't even seem to care which one I picked as long as I kept the wealth among other old-money families.

Not that I had any intention of dating any of them or taking over the business for that matter. One day, they would get that through their skulls. I hoped.

I just shook my head and hopped into the first cab I saw. I grinned a little as I passed my mother's limousine.

It took me under thirty minutes to get into the office, even without my parents' goddamn limo. Which was fortunate because I was there a good hour before everyone else arrived. It was the only way I would get through all the work piling up on my desk. The fundraising banquet was our biggest event thus far, and it would set the tone for the campaign season. And that was on top of everything else that was on my plate.

I'd been under a pile of paperwork for who even knew how long when a text hit my phone.

Are we still on for coffee later?

"Fuck," I grumbled.

I had completely forgotten that my friend Anna English was coming into town today, and I had promised her coffee. That was before I'd known how swamped I'd be with the banquet. But English lived in Los Angeles, and I never saw her anymore. I couldn't just bail.

"Ugh," I groaned again. I'd have to figure it out.

Yes! I might be a few minutes late.

When aren't you, babe?

I laughed. At least she understood.

"Ready for the fundraising department meeting, boss?" my assistant, Aspen, asked, popping her head into my office. Her long platinum-blonde hair fell like a waterfall over one shoulder, framing her pale skin and sky-blue eyes.

I checked the time. Somehow, two hours had already passed.

"All set," I lied.

"Okay! Let me know if you need anything else from me."

Aspen was a godsend. I'd gone through so many assistants before finding her. She was always eager to learn, which I'd found out was not a common trait among campaign assistants.

"Will do," I told her.

I grabbed everything I would need for the meeting off of my desk and stumbled into the conference room, scattering papers on the giant table. I arranged them into a neat pile, perfectly ready for this meeting. Even if I would have felt more comfortable after another twenty hours of prep.

Not that I had twenty extra hours. Not as the deputy campaign manager, where I had to oversee all six major departments—fundraising, communications, field, legal, tech, and political. I could spend every day on just one of these areas and not get enough done. But since the mayor's banquet was the most important thing on the agenda, this meeting was at the top of the list. And I was going to be sure that it went off without a hitch.

"Hey, girlfriend," Demi said as she entered the room.

Demi was the head of the fundraising department and probably my favorite person in the office. She was a short, curvy black woman from Brooklyn, who always seemed perfectly put together. In fact, she carried her own papers in a notebook with each person's name labeled on the front and a presentation board with every banquet guest's name on a sticky note.

"Morning, Demi."

"Aspen said you came in early again. Are you always going to show us up?" she asked with a grin. She set the board down on the table and then turned to face me, twirling a short corkscrew curl around her finger.

"Too much to do, so little time," I told her with a shrug. "I'm just going to grab my laptop. We can get started once everyone else is ready."

"Sounds good."

I hastened back to my office and grabbed my MacBook, pulling up the figures I had been looking at yesterday.

"Oh, hey, Lark. Do you have a minute?"

I glanced up to see Kelly from HR, peeking into the office. "Um, I have, like, three minutes before my meeting."

"Perfect! I'm trying to introduce the new attorney we just hired to everyone."

"You finally filled the position?" I asked in surprise.

We'd been searching for a while for someone with the proper qualifications in campaign finance. I hadn't thought it would be hard to find someone like that in New York City. Didn't everyone have a JD here?

"Yep! Come meet him real quick. I sent him to get coffee."

I shut my laptop and passed Kelly as she sank her hip against Aspen's desk and started chatting. Clearly, this *meet the new guy* thing was an excuse to chitchat, but I really *did* like to know everyone who worked here.

I stepped into the break room just as the new guy turned from the crappy coffeemaker. Our eyes met. Time slowed. Then froze. For the first time, I understood the meaning of my heart skipping a beat. Because it did.

I took in the deep dark brown orbs. Let my eyes crash over the swish of brown hair, the lethal cut of his jawline, the Cupid's bow of his perfect lips. That body. Holy fuck, the way that body filled out that black suit. And those hands. Builder's hands.

A part of me ached to step forward.

A part of me remembered what had happened.

How we had fallen apart all those years ago.

"Lark?" he asked in disbelief.

My traitorous heart fluttered.

"Hi, Sam."

To continue reading, grab *Cruel Truth* now!

ACKNOWLEDGMENTS

This book would not exist save for the six months I spent on the 2012 presidential election in 2012 at UNC-Chapel Hill and the week I spent in Madison during the 2018 primary. Both experiences are dear to my heart and breathe life into the characters and experiences within the walls of this story. So thank you every person that I worked with on campaign that made writing about those experiences possible. And every other person who helped bring this book from an idea into a reality. You're the unsung heroes.

We always like to see the happy ending to the madness. Campaign life is hard work. Living after campaign work is sometimes harder. So, I hope you, dear reader, continue on to read the rest of Lark and Sam's story in The Lying Season! Thanks for reading!

ABOUT THE AUTHOR

 K.A. Linde is the *USA Today* bestselling author of more than thirty novels. She has a Masters degree in political science from the University of Georgia, was the head campaign worker for the 2012 presidential campaign at UNC-Chapel Hill, and served as the head coach of the Duke University dance team.

She loves reading fantasy novels, traveling, baking insane desserts, and dancing in her spare time. She currently lives in Lubbock, Texas, with her husband and two super-adorable puppies.

Visit her online: www.kalinde.com

Or Facebook, Instagram, Twitter, & Tiktok:
@authorkalinde

For exclusive content: www.kalinde.com/subscribe